Matchmade Marriages

Will love be found through a Season in town?

Five young women from good families—
but reduced circumstances—are brought together
at Lady Mountjoy's home near Bath so that she
can choose which of them should accompany her
to London for the Season. These women—some
reluctant, some eager, some shy—are introduced
to fashionable Society life. But how much will
this help them find their perfect match?

Read Charlotte's story in
The Marquess Meets His Match

And Eliza's story in
A Pretend Match for the Viscount

Available now!

Author Note

There is something rather magical about the Regency era. Every year there are hundreds, perhaps even thousands, of books set among the ballrooms and the country estates of the wealthy, yet still there is an appetite for more. The clothes are elegant, reputations are everything and the dance of courtship plays out under the eyes of many. I love this period more than any other. When I close my eyes, I can picture the opulence of the country ballrooms and hear the musicians play the first note of a waltz or a quadrille.

A Pretend Match for the Viscount is set largely in London and I have tried to put all my favorite elements of an upper-class Regency London into the story. There are ballrooms aplenty, gorgeous dresses, striking riding habits and even a spot of ice-skating in St. James's Park. I hope you enjoy the escape to Regency London.

LAURA MARTIN

A Pretend Match for the Viscount

Recycling programs for this product may not exist in your area.

ISBN-13: 978-1-335-72337-6

A Pretend Match for the Viscount

Harlequin Enterprises ULC
22 Adelaide St. West, 41st Floor
Toronto, Ontario M5H 4E3, Canada
www.Harlequin.com

Printed in U.S.A.

Laura Martin writes historical romances with an adventurous undercurrent. When not writing, she spends her time working as a doctor in Cambridgeshire, where she lives with her husband. In her spare moments Laura loves to lose herself in a book and has been known to read from cover to cover in a single day when the story is particularly gripping. She also loves to travel—especially to visit historical sites and far-flung shores.

Books by Laura Martin

Harlequin Historical

A Ring for the Pregnant Debutante
An Unlikely Debutante
An Earl to Save Her Reputation
The Viscount's Runaway Wife
The Brooding Earl's Proposition
Her Best Friend, the Duke
One Snowy Night with Lord Hauxton
The Captain's Impossible Match

Matchmade Marriages

The Marquess Meets His Match
A Pretend Match for the Viscount

The Ashburton Reunion

Flirting with His Forbidden Lady
Falling for His Practical Wife

Scandalous Australian Bachelors

Courting the Forbidden Debutante
Reunited with His Long-Lost Cinderella
Her Rags-to-Riches Christmas

Visit the Author Profile page
at Harlequin.com for more titles.

For my wonderful editor, Linda.
Your gentle guidance has meant so
much to me over the years and shaped
every one of my books.

Chapter One

Spinning in a circle, Eliza tipped her head back and looked up at the ceiling. High above her an ornate chandelier sparkled with the light of one hundred candles, the flames glinting off the mirrored ceiling and making the whole room appear to be of another world. The ballroom was just starting to fill with people, with more guests arriving every few minutes, and Eliza felt a deep thrum of excitement pass through her body. *This* was what she had been waiting for her whole life. Tonight was the first true night of her London Season, the night where the rest of her life began.

'You look happy, Eliza,' Lucy said as she came and slipped her arm through her friend's.

'I am happy. Isn't this just the most wonderful thing you've ever experienced?'

Lucy smiled at her indulgently. Eliza knew her friend didn't share her overt enthusiasm for the Season, but Lucy would never do anything to dampen her spirits.

'Have you seen Lord Wilson?' Eliza raised herself up on to her toes to get a better view of the room. She had never minded her petite stature before she had come to London, but here it often meant she was straining to be able to see when the taller of her companions had an easy view.

'No.' Lucy paused and then stepped in a little closer. 'Be careful with him, he has a wicked reputation.'

'It's all just gossip, you know how the *ton* love to talk.'

'The rumours must be based on something.'

Eliza shook her head. 'Don't worry about me, I know we're fresh from the country, but I have more common sense than most of these debutantes who have been brought up in their gilded mansions.'

Lucy nodded, looking as though she wanted to say more, but eventually pressed her lips together.

'Let's take a walk around the room. I want to remember every detail of tonight.'

Arm in arm they weaved their way through the swelling crowd of people. There were only a few people Eliza recognised, smiling in greeting as they passed. They had been in London for a total of four weeks, but this was their first real ball. Lady Mountjoy, the kind and effusive woman who had brought Eliza to London from Somerset to experience the joys of the London Season along with three other young debutantes, had wanted them to settle in before launching them into society. The start of their Season had also been delayed by a short trip back to Somerset to be part of the wedding of a friend to Lady Mountjoy's nephew. Tonight was their first ball, their formal launch into society, but the past few weeks hadn't been wasted. Lady Mountjoy had ensured they were seen strolling through Hyde

Park or taking tea with some of the influential members of society. There had even been one or two dinner parties and this was where Eliza had met Lord Wilson.

'There he is,' she almost squealed with joy, but was just in time to make sure her expression was fixed into a serene smile before he glanced in her direction.

Lord Wilson acknowledged her with a smile and Eliza felt her heart soar as he excused himself from the group he was with and strode over to greet her. Lucy murmured something Eliza didn't quite catch and faded away into the background.

'You're looking rather lovely tonight, Miss Stanley,' Lord Wilson said, bending over her hand. 'Tell me you've saved the first dance for me.'

Eliza felt a surge of anticipation as he looked at her with expectant eyes and she knew this was what she was made for. Her life had seemed incomplete when she was in Somerset: it had been as though she didn't quite belong. Here, now, this was where she was meant to be.

'Of course, Lord Wilson, I couldn't let my first dance be with anyone else.

As they turned, a man brushed against her. It was more her fault than his, but all the same he stopped and apologised.

'My apologies,' he said, his voice low and so quiet she could barely hear it over the noise of the ball.

'Have a mind where you step, Thannock,' Lord Wilson said.

Eliza saw the other man regard Lord Wilson coolly before turning on his heel and striding off across the ballroom.

* * *

Samuel, Lord Thannock, looked at his pocket watch and wondered if anyone would notice if he slipped away now. Surely forty-five minutes was plenty of time to spend at one of these events. It wasn't as though he were good company and he had already spent a little time with the host and hostess.

Careful not to make eye contact with any of the hopeful debutantes standing around the edge of the ballroom, he headed for the door and breathed a sigh of relief once he was free from the crowds. It was quieter out in the grand hallway with all of the guests now arrived and either in the ballroom or the drawing room off to one side, playing cards. He hadn't brought a coat, knowing early in the evening he would want to make a swift exit once his obligations were fulfilled.

He turned right out of the ballroom, heading towards the front door, but before he could step out into the cold night air he heard something that made him pause.

Somewhere behind him he heard the deep voice of a man followed by an uncertain giggle of a young woman.

'Come on, no one will see.'

'We should get back.'

'One minute, I promise.'

Sam didn't want to see who it was—the couple would prefer privacy for their illicit liaison and he certainly did not want to become embroiled in their secret. He took another step towards the door and the woman's voice rang out again. This time there was something in her tone that didn't sound quite right.

'I think we should go back to the ballroom.'

'Shhh, someone will hear us and then you'll be ruined.'

There was a short moment of silence and then Sam felt a wave of revulsion break over him as he heard the panicked cry of a young woman. He had never been a man to get involved in matters that did not concern him, but with something like this he didn't hesitate. Turning back from the front door, he crossed the hall in a few steps, listening carefully for some clue as to where the couple had secreted themselves. There was a sharp intake of breath and the sound of a cry being smothered as Sam started to throw open doors.

The couple were in the third room he tried, the woman squashed underneath her companion who had his back to the door. He caught a glimpse of her petrified face, her eyes wide and her mouth obscured by a large hand.

He crossed the room in a second, not giving the man a chance to realise he and the young lady were no longer alone. Gripping the man by the collar, Sam wrenched him away from the woman and threw him backwards, watching with satisfaction as he stumbled and fell to the floor.

'Are you hurt?' He took in the sight of the young woman in front of him, dress crumpled and brows furrowed, a look of pure panic in her eyes. Instinctively, he reached out, wanting to comfort her, but caught himself in time. The last thing she would want would be for another man to touch her.

'What the hell are you doing here, Thannock?' Lord Wilson spat as he scrambled up from the floor.

Sam ignored him—he'd always found Wilson to be insufferable and rude, but he hadn't thought he was capable of this.

'Do you want me to get someone for you?'

The young woman shook her head, pulling herself upright.

'You're sticking your nose in where it's not wanted, Thannock. Leave me and Miss Stanley in peace.'

Sam rounded on the young Viscount, using his superior size to tower over the other man.

'Get out,' he said, his voice quiet but steely. 'Get out and stay out.'

'I don't take orders from you.'

Sam took a step forward and Lord Wilson involuntarily flinched away. For a long moment he hesitated and then headed for the door, pausing when he was almost out of the room.

'Don't fool yourself you could have had any more than this, Miss Stanley—you're good for a quick fumble, but we are from different worlds.'

Watching the young woman's expression, he saw Lord Wilson's words hit a nerve, but she valiantly tried to hide it, exhaling in relief once the Viscount was out of the room.

For a long moment she closed her eyes and took a few deep, shuddering breaths, the colour slowly returning to her cheeks.

'Miss Stanley, is it?' He didn't recognise her, apart from being the young woman he had knocked into earlier in the evening. The name was vaguely familiar and he wondered if she was one of the debutantes Lady Mountjoy had brought to London for the Season.

She was pretty, even in her dishevelled state. Petite in build with dark hair that curled about her shoulders where it had sprung loose from the intricate hairstyle she had worn earlier in the evening. There was a vitality in her green eyes that made him want to stare into them, but he caught himself before he looked for too long.

'Yes. Thank you.'

Sam nodded in acknowledgement, watching carefully as she pulled at her dress, straightening it. She was doing her best to look as though nothing had just happened, but there were subtle signs, things you might miss if you didn't know where to look, that she was barely holding on to her composure.

He glanced at the door, wondering if she would prefer him to leave, then reprimanded himself silently. *He* would prefer to leave, he hated any sort of drama, but here was a woman in need and he couldn't call himself a gentleman if he walked away.

'Sit down,' he said gruffly. 'Take a minute.'

'I'm fine.'

'You're shaking.'

Miss Stanley looked down at her hands as if they were mystical objects and then sank into the cushions of the sofa. Sam didn't know the Mountjoys' London residence all that well, but the houses of the wealthy were similar enough that once you'd been in half a dozen you could normally navigate them pretty easily. His eyes darting across the shelves, he found what he was looking for—a decanter of brandy and two crystal glasses.

'Here.' He poured out two generous measures of the amber liquid and handed one glass to Miss Stanley, surprised when she threw it back in one gulp, grimac-

ing a little at the burn in her throat, but not coughing
or spluttering.

'You must think I'm an utter fool,' Miss Stanley said
eventually, glancing up at him momentarily before her
gaze returned resolutely to her lap.

Remembering his father's advice to always count
to three before criticising someone else, he paused and
then shook his head.

'Lord Wilson is the only one in the wrong,' he said
quietly. 'You shouldn't have to fear being alone with
anyone, to doubt their intentions.'

She nodded, the tears forming in her eyes, but she
brushed them away quickly.

'I am a fool, but you're kind to say otherwise.'

Sam had been pacing backwards and forward in
front of her, eager to be gone, eager to move on from
Miss Stanley and return to the solitude of his house, but
something in her tone made him stop and slowly ease
himself on to the sofa next to her. He was careful not
to sit too close and for a long moment they just shared
the silence together.

Sam was searching for something reassuring to say
when they both stiffened at a noise at the door. Lord
Wilson had slammed the door to the study closed when
he had departed, but now there was the unmistakable
click of the handle turning. There were voices outside,
too, men laughing and talking.

In an instant, Sam felt his body tense as if his in-
stincts were getting him ready to flee, but there was
nowhere to run. Here he was in a dark room with a dishevelled young lady. They might be sitting innocently

on the sofa, but that wouldn't save them from the scandal of being found alone together.

Miss Stanley looked as panicked as he felt and half rose from the sofa as if considering hiding behind a potted plant or underneath the mahogany desk.

The voices outside swelled, but the handle didn't turn any more and Sam wondered if maybe they would be lucky.

'We need to hide,' Miss Stanley whispered.

'There is nowhere to hide.'

'Behind the curtains.'

'They'll see our feet.'

'Under the desk?'

'And if they look underneath? We will look guilty.'

'We have to try *something*.'

Sam had thought himself immune to beseeching looks and imploring tones, but something in her eyes struck him in the chest and he found himself nodding decisively despite it being against his better judgement. It would be better if they placed themselves on opposite sides of the room and tried to look as uninterested in one another as possible. Either that or for Miss Stanley to make a run for it, to slip out of the door with her head down and hope no one recognised her.

Instead, he found himself directing Miss Stanley to the heavy curtains as she had suggested, motioning for her to climb up on the windowsill and lift her feet from the ground. He did the same, acutely aware of how her legs pressed against his as they huddled together.

'Mountjoy said there was another pack of cards on the writing desk,' a male voice rang out a few seconds later as the door opened and the noise from the ball-room grew louder.

Sam did not attend church every Sunday, but now he closed his eyes and prayed that the men would find the cards and get out before either he or Miss Stanley did something to give themselves away.

'Hurry up, I'm on a lucky streak and I don't want to miss my chance of bleeding you dry for once.'

'Got them.'

Relief spread through Sam as he heard the foot-steps crossing the floorboards. Perhaps Miss Stanley had been right to insist they hide. He glanced over at his companion and watched in horror as she toppled from the narrow windowsill, her dress too silky to give her much purchase. She went forward through the curtains, letting out a small, stifled cry as she landed on the floor.

'What on earth is happening?' one of the men ex-claimed, more amused than anything else.

'Please,' he heard Miss Stanley say, 'pretend I'm not here.' He had to applaud her audacity and for a moment it seemed as though the gentlemen might contemplate granting her request, then he heard more voices at the door and a gasp of horror.

Knowing he couldn't let her face the accusing looks in the growing crowd alone, he stepped out from be-hind the curtain and helped Miss Stanley to her feet.

There were three men in the doorway and as he straightened a group of older women came into view. At first there was a shocked hush and then a murmur of disapproval. Sam set his shoulders back and took a step forward, meaning to shield Miss Stanley from the admonishing stares. With a light touch on his arm she drew his attention and shook her head and he felt a flicker of admiration. A scandal he could withstand, but it would likely be the end of any high hopes Miss Stanley might have fostered for the Season. She would be whispered about over the weeks and months that followed.

'There you are,' their hostess's voice rang out as she sailed past the gathering crowd into the study. 'I'm sorry, I know I said I would join you five minutes ago, but I lost track of time.' She stared around as if only just noticing the gawping group of people. With an air of casual excitement she motioned to a woman Sam vaguely recognised and said in a loud whisper, 'They're finalising the details of their engagement. I do love wedding plans.'

Sam swallowed hard, wondering if there was less air in the room than there had been a few seconds ago. His lungs were burning and he wanted to take in great gulps of air to try to breathe, but a steely glance from Lady Mountjoy was enough to prompt him to instead smile serenely.

'Shall we sit down, my dears, we have so much to talk about.'

Lady Mountjoy sat in the middle of the sofa, patting the cushions on either side, and like two well-controlled puppets Sam and Miss Stanley sat down.

Chapter Two

Eliza didn't ever cry, or at least she hadn't for more than a decade. Crying was a waste of time. It didn't achieve anything other than to make her eyes look puffy and signal a weakness to anyone who witnessed the outlet of emotion. When she was ten she had cried over some trivial matter, something that would be forgotten the next day. She could remember some of the girls from the village pointing and laughing at her and for the next week they had made little crying noises whenever she had come near. It had shown Eliza that any show of weakness could be used to hurt you and it was better to keep those sorts of emotions inside.

Today she had been close to breaking her no-crying rule at least four times and it wasn't yet past noon.

With a shudder, she remembered Lord Wilson's hands on her, the weight of his body pressed against hers. She'd felt the heat of his breath on her neck and in that moment realised she was helpless to do anything to stop him. It had been a sobering thought, that sense of helplessness, a feeling she never wanted to experience again.

Closing her eyes, she leaned her forehead against the windowpane and revelled in the coldness of the glass. Soon she would be summoned downstairs where her future would be decided and all her dreams shattered in one fell swoop.

'It may not be as bad as you think,' Jane said softly. Jane Ashworth was another of the debutantes Lady Mountjoy had brought to London from Somerset for a Season. She was quiet, softly spoken and intellectual. Eliza knew they were opposites in most ways, but that did not stop her from treasuring Jane's companionship. Her calm demeanour was often a soothing balm to the knocks Eliza picked up as she hurtled through the world.

'Lady Mountjoy announced we were finalising our engagement,' Eliza said glumly.

'Lord Thannock seems pleasant,' Jane said.

'Hmmm.' *That* was part of the problem. He had seemed pleasant, and she would be thankful for ever that he'd come to her rescue, but Eliza didn't want to be forced into marriage with a pleasant man. That had been exactly the reason she had been so keen to escape from Somerset. Her parents had planned out her whole life for her, marriage to a respectable gentleman followed by a life of dullness as a wife and mother. It wasn't what she wanted. She wanted adventure, she wanted excitement.

'Lady Mountjoy has a way of sorting things out,' Lucy said from her spot on the bed. The three of them had been waiting for Lord Thannock for the past hour, wondering when he would make an appearance.

'She was very kind last night. She promised she would help us work everything out and then sent me upstairs and Lord Thannock home to get some rest.' Eliza shook her head. 'I just wish I knew what she was planning.'

'Lord Thannock has arrived,' Miss Huntley announced as she burst into the room. Miss Huntley was the fourth and final debutante in their little group and Eliza had trouble hiding her dislike for the cold young woman. Whereas Eliza, Jane and Lucy were firm friends, Miss Huntley had rejected every gesture of friendship and preferred to keep to herself. She had never even invited the other young women to use her first name despite their all living together for months. 'Lady Mountjoy has asked for your presence in the drawing room.'

Eliza stood, smoothing down her skirts, and took a moment to check herself in the mirror. She was not looking to make a conquest of Lord Thannock, but it wouldn't hurt to look her best. Grimacing, she looked away quickly—a sleepless night meant she had dark circles under her eyes and her cheeks were pale and colourless.

'Good luck,' Miss Huntley said, 'I'm not sure what Lady Mountjoy can do for you—the rumours were rife last night and it had only just happened.'

Eliza managed to resist reverting to a five-year-old version of herself and sticking out her tongue, opting instead to brush past Miss Huntley in what she hoped was a regal manner.

Her bedroom that she shared with Jane was up three flights of stairs and the long walk down gave her enough opportunity to compose herself so that when she entered the drawing room at least she had stopped her hands from shaking.

Lord Thannock was standing by the window, his bearing stiff and his clothes formal. He looked as though he were about to attend a funeral and his expression matched his sombre attire.

Turning around as she entered, he gave her a nod of greeting, but didn't approach. Eliza hesitated for a moment and then perched on the edge of one of the armchairs, wishing Lady Mountjoy would hurry up and tell her what the future would hold.

'How are you today, Miss Stanley?' Lord Thannock said eventually. His voice was deep but quiet, and she glanced over at him, properly looking at him for the first time. Although she was no expert in the intricacies of society, Eliza was quick and observant and had already worked out there were different groups among the younger gentlemen of the *ton*.

First were the peacocks, gentlemen like Lord Wilson who dressed extravagantly and were perfectly coiffed. They were sharp and prided themselves on their charm and their wit. Next were the followers, men who wished they were more like the peacocks and hung on their every word. The last group was considerably smaller and made up of men like Lord Thannock. They were quieter but in no way shy, so confident in themselves and their opinions they didn't feel the need to make a fuss. Successful men who were not weighed down by the opinions of others.

She opened her mouth to reply, but thankfully was saved by the arrival of Lady Mountjoy. It probably would be frowned upon to tell one's possible future husband that the last twelve hours had been the worst of her entire life.

'Ah, I am so glad you are here, Sam. What a mess we've got ourselves into.'

Eliza blinked at the familiarity between Lady Mountjoy and Lord Thannock. She greeted him with the warmth many people would reserve for a son or a treasured nephew.

'Lord Mountjoy has been held up by a matter of business but will try to join us soon if he can. You look well, Sam, recent events notwithstanding.'

'I am well, thank you. Or at least I was.'

Eliza bristled. She didn't expect him to be jumping for joy at the thought of the scandal that engulfed them, but he didn't need to be so open in his disdain.

'Yes, the unfortunate events of last night,' Lady Mountjoy said, levelling them both with a steady gaze. 'What on earth happened?'

Eliza cleared her throat, a wave of heat spreading through her body followed by a pulse of nausea. How could she have been so foolish?

'I stepped away from the ball, Lady Mountjoy, and then found myself in the unfortunate position of being left alone with a gentleman.'

'With Lord Thannock?' Lady Mountjoy looked momentarily confused. It would seem she viewed the Viscount as an example of good moral character.

'No,' Eliza said quickly. 'Another gentleman.'

'Oh, Eliza, what have you got yourself mixed up in?'

She was surprised when Lord Thannock spoke up, as direct and to the point as she had expected him to be. 'Lord Wilson tried to force himself on Miss Stanley. I pulled him off.'

Lady Mountjoy gasped and then moved so she was sitting next to Eliza. 'Oh, my dear, I didn't realise. How terrible for you.'

'I know I shouldn't have been alone with him.'

'No,' Lord Thannock murmured. 'You shouldn't. Perhaps we wouldn't be in this mess if you'd thought a little more.'

'You're blaming me?'

'I'm saying it was foolish to agree to go into a darkened room with a scoundrel like Lord Wilson. I am not blaming you for what happened next, that lays squarely on Wilson's shoulders.'

'Oh. Good.' She dropped her own shoulders and straightened her back. It would appear Lord Thannock wasn't afraid to speak his mind. All last night she had tossed and turned, trying to think of the best way out of this awful situation, but she hadn't once considered Lord Thannock might be trying to do the same. It was her reputation that would be left in tatters, her hopes and dreams that would be dashed.

'That absolute cad. I've always found him objectionable, but to think a viscount would do something so terrible,' Lady Mountjoy said, looking at her with pity in her eyes.

'He won't bother you again,' Lord Thannock said with a certainty that perplexed Eliza. Surely he couldn't know that for sure.

'You can't know that.'

Lord Thannock fixed the full force of his gaze on her and for a moment Eliza felt everything else fade into the background. He was an attractive man, with thick brown hair and eyes so dark they almost looked black. She tried not to squirm under the intensity of his attention, but it was hard when his eyes were fixed on hers unwaveringly.

'I went to see Lord Wilson this morning,' he said quietly. 'He will not be bothering you again. He has a family issue to sort out in Yorkshire and I doubt he will be back for a month or two.'

'You went to see him this morning?'

'Yes.'

'To tell him to keep away?'

'Yes.'

'And he agreed? Just like that?'

Lord Thannock shrugged as if he would be more shocked if Lord Wilson hadn't agreed to do exactly what he'd told him to.

'Thank you, Sam, that will be a weight off Miss Stanley's mind, I'm sure.'

Eliza nodded, surreptitiously scrutinising the Viscount. She'd heard him being gossiped about during her few weeks in London—he was a very eligible bachelor after all. Most people seemed to think he was distant, aloof, unobtainable, with one young woman remarking his air of uninterest made him even more desirable. Everyone wanted to be the one to finally spark Lord Thannock's interest.

'By now everyone in London will be aware you were alone together in the study,' Lady Mountjoy said, and Eliza saw her glancing at Lord Thannock. Eliza hadn't realised quite how at the mercy of the Viscount she was. She'd come downstairs thinking she was going to have to fight for her future, but from the furrow on Lady Mountjoy's normally smooth brow she was fast understanding that she would have to take whatever Lord Thannock offered. The idea left a bitter taste in her mouth.

'One solution would be for you two to get engaged,' Lady Mountjoy said quietly.

Eliza wasn't sure who protested first, but Lord Thannock was certainly the loudest.

'That is not going to happen,' he said, shaking his head with an air of finality. 'I am open to anything else to help Miss Stanley salvage some of her reputation, but I will not marry her.'

'*I* also do not wish to marry Lord Thannock,' Eliza said quickly, feeling a little hurt that he was dismissing her so quickly. She didn't want to marry him, but he didn't need to be so brutal in his assessment of her as a potential wife. She'd always thought she wouldn't struggle to find a husband when the time came to settle down.

'That's settled then,' Lord Thannock said with twitch of a smile on his lips. 'We don't want to marry.'

'No,' Lady Mountjoy said slowly, 'but Miss Stanley is

in a very difficult position. Her prospects will be severely damaged if we do nothing, and although I think we can all agree she was a little foolish stepping away from the ballroom with Lord Wilson, that shouldn't be enough to condemn her to a year of being shunned by society.'

Lord Thannock remained silent, his face impossible to read, his expression impassive.

'I am aware neither of you wishes to marry and I agree it would be ridiculous to expect it for such a misunderstanding, but I wonder if there may be another solution.'

'Go on,' Lord Thannock said. Eliza felt herself leaning forward in her chair, wondering what Lady Mountjoy had come up with.

'An engagement,' she said, holding up their hands to silence their protests. 'Not a true one—I heard your objections the first time—but the ruse of one. A month, perhaps six weeks, where you pretend to be engaged. Miss Stanley will be the woman who has captured the elusive Lord Thannock's attention and when the time is right you will drift apart.'

'When the time is right?'

'Yes. Once there is another scandal, something bigger, more gossipworthy. Or when she has sparked the interest of another gentleman.'

Eliza closed her eyes for a moment. It wasn't how she had imagined the first month of her Season to go, but she couldn't deny it was a good idea. If it worked it would mean she got to stay in London and hopefully experience all the things she had dreamed about these past few months.

'I know it is a lot to ask, Sam,' Lady Mountjoy said quietly, 'but this is Miss Stanley's reputation, her whole future, in jeopardy.'

After a long pause, Lord Thannock nodded, and Eliza felt a strange mix of relief and trepidation.

'Good. I'll leave you two lovebirds to settle the details,' she said with a clap of her hands, standing and sailing from the room.

Sam looked at the young woman sitting across from him and wondered how he had allowed himself to get lumbered with a fiancée. Even a fake fiancée was more commitment than he was ready to take on. Especially a fake fiancée like Miss Eliza Stanley.

'Hopefully there will be a momentous scandal very soon,' Miss Stanley muttered, starting to chew on her nails, but then seeming to catch herself and force her hands into her lap.

'You seem less than thrilled about the prospect of an engagement,' he said quietly, trying to suppress the smile that was tugging at the corner of his lips. He couldn't find it in himself to feel offended at her reluctance. He might not know her reasons for not being excited by the prospect of being tied to him socially for the next few weeks, but he felt the same. He was an eligible bachelor, but he was not what everyone wanted and it would appear Miss Stanley had set her sights on a different Season from how this was unfolding.

'This is not how it is meant to be,' Miss Stanley said morosely.

'Oh?'

She looked at him with those intense green eyes and vehemently shook her head. 'I was just starting to feel free, as if someone had opened my cage and I was stretching my wings ready to fly and now I'm trapped again.'

'It is just a few weeks, Miss Stanley,' he said, aware of how dismissive he sounded. 'Then no one will be stopping you from flying away.'

'I don't want to fly away,' she said with a sigh, 'I want to fly right into the middle of everything.'

Sam watched as she stood and restlessly paced around the room as if she found it hard to settle, hard to remain still. He was getting the feeling the next few weeks were going to test his patience, as he was fast realising he and Miss Stanley were opposite in so many ways. He thought of his house in the country, his idyllic escape, his refuge from the hustle and bustle of the city. He'd planned to head there at the end of the week and spend a fortnight away from the capital before his responsibilities called him back. It looked as though that would be out of the question.

'How do you want to approach this?'

'What do you mean?'

He stood, pacing towards the window and looking out for a moment. The street was busy, filled with activity as the morning was fast becoming afternoon. It made him feel restless, as if he wanted to get out of here and walk until his legs gave out from underneath him.

'I think we should keep our public appearances to a minimum. Allow Lady Mountjoy to let it be known we are engaged, but give people the opportunity to forget about us and the scandal from last night.'

'That's ridiculous,' Miss Stanley said, screwing up her nose. 'We need to be out there, to be seen. To show everyone we are not ashamed and hiding away.'

'How will that help?'

'I am hardly going to find another gentleman who wants to marry me sitting in Lady Mountjoy's drawing room, am I?'

He had to concede she had a point, although he wasn't sure it was the real reason Miss Stanley wanted to be out in society rather than lying low. She was the type to flourish in the glow of attention, to revel in the whirl of balls and parties. He couldn't have found someone so completely different to him if he'd tried.

'Perhaps a few engagements together would be acceptable,' he said quietly.

'We should be seen together today, looking as if we hadn't even considered there might be gossip about us.'

'I can't today. Prior arrangement,' he barked, standing abruptly. He felt as if a noose was closing around his neck and he needed to escape into the fresh air. There was no prior arrangement, but he couldn't give Miss Stanley what she wanted today. It was enough that he had agreed to this outrageous scheme of Lady Mountjoy's to pretend to be engaged to the young woman, he would allow himself a little time to mull over everything that had happened before he stepped out into the world with her.

Before she could protest, he moved towards the door, only turning back when his hand was on the handle.

'Good day, Miss Stanley. I will see you soon.'

Chapter Three

Eliza surreptitiously checked over both her shoulders before crossing the street and ascending the steps to the smart town house that sat on the end of the row overlooking a small gated park. She didn't know many people in London yet, but it would be just her luck if one of the few people she did know saw her approaching Lord Thannock's house when already their names were linked in scandal.

'Stupid man,' she muttered. If he had been less reluctant to step into the role of her fiancé for a few weeks she wouldn't have to be here, risking her reputation all over again. It had been three days, three long and dull days, since they had agreed to pretend to be engaged and in that time she had heard nothing from the man.

It was infuriating. The night before Jane, Lucy and Miss Huntley had all hurried away to a wonderful ball and she had been left sitting home alone wondering what she was missing, all because Lord Thannock hadn't confirmed if he would be in attendance. They needed at least their first outing to be together, to confirm they were legitimately engaged and the whispers about them being found together would fade away.

She had resolved not to miss another event so here she was, head bent with the hood of her cloak shadowing her face, creeping through Mayfair in pursuit of a man she barely knew. It wasn't how she thought her first weeks of her Season would be spent—whenever she had pictured it she'd always thought the gentlemen would be pursuing *her*.

Quickly, she rapped on the door, hopping from foot to foot as she waited for someone to answer. It seemed to take for ever for the door to open and a footman to peer out at her.

'Miss Eliza Stanley here to see Lord Thannock,' she said, inching forward.

The footman looked surprised, as if Lord Thannock didn't get many guests, but quickly recovered. 'I shall see if he is in, Miss Stanley.'

The door began to close and for an instant Eliza was too incredulous to move. Surely she wasn't going to be made to wait on the doorstep like a delivery boy. Before the door could close fully she lunged forward, darting inside much to the surprise of the footman.

'I'll just wait in here for him,' she said with a sweet smile, her heart hammering away in her chest.

After a moment's hesitation the young man headed off down the hallway, leaving her to look around more openly in awe.

Inside the house was huge, stretching back beyond a sweeping staircase. Eliza tried not to gawp, thinking of her parents' modest house just outside Bath. They weren't poor, but without Lady Mountjoy's kindness there was no way she would ever have seen the interior of a house as grand as this one. Grander even than Lady Mountjoy's.

The footman reappeared, looking harried, and directed her to a drawing room with views over the gardens beyond. Eliza perched on the edge of a chair, her bottom barely touching the upholstery before the door was flung open again and Lord Thannock strode in.

'What are you doing here?'

'Good afternoon,' she said, treating him to her most dazzling smile. 'How are you today, Lord Thannock?'

He was not to be distracted. 'What are you doing here, Miss Stanley?'

'I've come to visit my fiancé.'

'You can't do that.' He shook his head. 'Surely you know you can't be here.'

Of course she did and for the first time Eliza started to doubt her plan. What if instead of forcing him into spending time with her it made him pull out of their arrangement?

'You are not lacking in intelligence, Miss Stanley,' he said quietly, and she could see a flash of anger in his eyes, 'so you cannot blame being stupid. What on earth made you think coming to my house was a good idea?'

'I've sent three notes,' Eliza said, refusing to be cowed by his hard stare, 'and you replied to none of them. You agree to act as my fiancé and then you disappear for days on end. What am I supposed to think?'

'Hardly days on end,' he muttered, but Eliza could see some of the annoyance had disappeared from his expression and he was no longer holding himself so stiffly. 'Three notes?'

'Yes. Three.'

He grunted and shook his head. 'That is a bit remiss of me, but it doesn't mean you can come *unchaperoned* to my front door.'

'People are gossiping and I am left to hide away in my bedroom, not knowing if you are going to renege on your promise to help me. I had to do something.'

'I wouldn't go back on a promise like that.'

'How am I supposed to know that? We barely know one another.'

'Coming here was irresponsible and risky.'

'At least you are talking to me now.'

'I've been busy,' he said quietly.

Eliza couldn't imagine what could keep him so busy as to completely neglect their agreement, but she conceded she didn't know much about the man. Perhaps he was guardian to eight boisterous children, or worked as a spy for Napoleon's forces, or had a secret second life as a prize-winning jockey. They would be decent excuses.

She was about to enquire further when a noise from above their heads made her pause. It sounded like the closing of a door and a peal of laughter. In itself the noise was nothing—it could have been a maid surprised in her duties or Lord Thannock's elderly aunt finding something amusing in the morning gossip column. What made her pause was Lord Thannock's reaction to the sound. He stiffened completely, and Eliza would wager every muscle in his body was held tense. After ten seconds he blinked, the only movement in an otherwise entirely still face.

'We should go for a walk,' he said after thirty seconds, seeming to recover enough to grind out the words.

Eliza glanced up, even though there was of course just the ceiling above their heads.

'A walk around the park—that sounds like a suitable outing for a newly engaged couple, does it not?' He did very well in hiding the note of desperation in his voice and if Eliza hadn't been so suspicious she might not have noticed it.

'A walk does sound lovely,' she said, drawing out her words and watching him become more and more agitated as they heard soft footsteps from above them.

Gripping her firmly by the elbow, he guided her up from the seat and across the room, passing the footman in the hall so quickly that the young man couldn't get to the door in time to open it before Lord Thannock had thrown it open himself.

Eliza glanced behind her, half hoping she might catch a glimpse of the woman who had caused Lord Thannock so much agitation. As the door started to close behind them, she heard a refined voice call out, 'Samuel.'

'Lovely day for a stroll,' Lord Thannock said much too loudly and much too cheerily, hurrying down the steps in front of his house and crossing the street before she had even turned back around. Eliza was forced to half run after him, noting how he only slowed when they were out of view of the house. 'Shall we head to St James's Park?'

Eliza barely had time to nod her head before he was off again, walking so fast there was no way they could converse and walk at the same time.

* * *

Sam knew he was walking too fast. Miss Stanley was only petite and she was having to work hard to keep up with him, but he had this urge to get as far away from the house as possible and he seemed unable to override it.

Only once they had shot through the gates to the park did he find he was able to slow down. St James's was his favourite park in London. Nowhere near as fashionable as the winding paths or riding routes of Hyde Park, there was something charming about this lesser-visited spot. When in London he would often escape from the noise of the city into the park and although it was no substitute for the rolling green hills of Sussex it was a pleasant interlude for ten minutes.

Trying to ignore the curious glances Miss Stanley was giving him, he offered her his arm. He knew she was relying on him to save her reputation and as such he expected she would brush over their rapid departure from his house, which suited him. The less he needed to explain about his guest the better.

'I don't mind,' Miss Stanley said eventually.

'What don't you mind?'

'If you have a mistress closeted in that big old house of yours.'

Sam missed his step, stumbling for a moment before righting himself.

'A mistress?'

'Yes. A mistress. A lover. A courtesan. Someone sharing your bed.'

Sam was a quiet man, reserving his words for when they mattered, but he wasn't often rendered speechless.

'I don't have a mistress.'

Miss Stanley shrugged. 'Whatever you say. *I'm* just saying I don't care one way or the other. I am not using this opportunity to get close to you, in the hope we might fall madly and passionately in love. This is purely a pretence for a few weeks until we can go our separate ways.'

'Good. I still don't have a mistress.'

She gave him a look that made him wonder what they taught young ladies in Somerset.

'I hope she isn't too upset with you,' Miss Stanley said quietly.

'*She* can't be upset with me because she does not exist.'

'There was someone upstairs. I heard them calling your name.'

Sam fell silent for a moment, running a hand through his hair. 'It was my mother,' he said eventually.

'Your mother?'

'Why is that so hard to believe?'

'I've never seen anyone so eager to pretend their mother was not in the house.'

Sam grimaced. It might sound cruel, but he often pretended his mother wasn't in the country, let alone the house.

'I didn't want you to meet her.'

'Oh.' Miss Stanley sounded hurt and as much as he wished he didn't have to be out strolling through St James's Park with a fake fiancée, he didn't want to hurt the young woman.

'Not because of you,' he said gruffly.

Miss Stanley frowned.

'My mother is…' He groped in the recesses of his mind for the right word to describe her. 'Difficult.' It hardly delved into the character of the vibrant, complex woman who was his mother, but he was hoping not to have to talk too much about her. With luck she would be on her way out of London in a few days, allowing the peace to return to his town house.

'Difficult?'

He turned to Miss Stanley with a smile that felt a little forced as he wondered how much to tell her. Hopefully they would spend a few short weeks together and no more, so she hardly needed his life story.

'I apologise for not contacting you sooner,' he said as they walked side by side past one of the ponds. 'I had every intention of suggesting we meet to clarify a strategy for these next few weeks, but then my mother arrived rather dramatically and unexpectedly.'

'She is not unwell, I hope?'

'No. She is the picture of health.' He sighed, feeling guilty for the thought that a mild head cold might keep his mother out of mischief for a few days. 'I do not mean for her to shoulder the blame for my inconsiderate behaviour, how I act is solely my responsibility, but…'

'Even as adults we are at the whim of our parents,' Miss Stanley said quietly.

He looked at her with interest, for the first time wondering what her story was. He knew Lady Mountjoy had collected this group of debutantes, women who would not otherwise have had the opportunity to experience a Season in London, and brought them here to enjoy the balls and the socialising, but he realised he had not stopped to consider what set Miss Stanley apart from the rest. He had been too quick to categorise her as just another foolish debutante, too easily charmed by the first man who showed a little interest.

As they reached a bench with views over the park and the city beyond he paused. He didn't need the complication of Miss Eliza Stanley in his life right now, but she *was* in it. He had agreed to help her and that meant making some time for the young woman.

'I think we need to discuss a plan for the coming weeks,' he said, motioning to the bench.

She sat, her posture rigid and her hand clasped tightly in her lap. She gave off the impression of a confident young woman, but he wondered how much of that was an act.

'Shall we negotiate?'

This made her smile, a faint tug at the corner of her lips.

'We need to attend everything and anything we are invited to,' she said, shifting towards him. 'Lady Mountjoy has made it very clear I need to garner the attention of a suitable gentleman to allow me to slip from this *engagement* to another offering for me if possible. I can only do that if I am out socialising.'

Sam grimaced. Socialising every night of the week sounded like his own personal hell.

'Two engagements per week, you get to choose which,' he offered.

'Two? That is ridiculous. Ten I could live with, although there would be the fear of missing out on some of the other events.'

'Ten?' he growled. That was more than he would expect to accept in three months. 'That's more than one a day.'

'I see you excel at mathematics, Lord Thannock,' she murmured.

'Even you cannot expect to attend more than one ball each evening.'

'I am not merely talking about balls. There are lunches, dinner parties, afternoon outings, carriage rides, the opera and the theatre, dances at the Assembly Rooms and, of course, balls.'

'I feel exhausted merely listening to all you wish to do.'

'Nonsense.'

'I will agree to four events throughout the week.'

'Eight would be acceptable to me as I suppose once the gossips are aware we are engaged we do not need to attend *everything* together.'

He eyed her, saw the unwavering determination in her eyes and felt a flicker of admiration for the annoying young woman beside him. She was far too caught up in the whirl of society, but he could appreciate a steely will when he saw one.

'Six is my final offer,' he said eventually, wondering if she would try to continue to negotiate. There must have been something in his eyes, for after a second of contemplation, she nodded.

They sat in silence for a while, both looking out over the lush green parkland.

'I would have accepted five,' Miss Stanley said after a minute.

'And I would have stretched to seven.'

She smiled at him then, a genuine smile filled with warmth, and Sam felt a jolt of attraction shoot through him. Suddenly, she looked more relaxed, as if this whole time she had been on edge, unsure of her position.

'I am sorry,' he said quietly. 'I understand the precarious position you are in and it was never my intention to add to your worries. I am no expert, but I do trust Lady Mountjoy, and if she thinks this the best way to preserve your reputation, then I believe you are in safe hands.'

Miss Stanley nodded and Sam could see there was something she was contemplating saying, something that she wasn't sure would be well received. He tried an encouraging smile, but when he saw Miss Stanley frown he wondered if it had come out more as a grimace.

'I wonder...' Miss Stanley said slowly and then shook her head.

'What do you wonder?'

'You don't think Lady Mountjoy is trying to make a match between us?'

Sam let out a short, sharp bark of laughter. 'Without a doubt. The woman is relentless in wanting everyone to be happily settled with a spouse and half a dozen children on the way.'

Miss Stanley looked horrified.

'I don't want to marry you and you don't want to marry me. Lady Mountjoy will come around to the fact in a few weeks,' Sam said reassuringly. 'She won't have a choice in the matter.'

Chapter Four

'Tell me everything,' Lucy said as she perched on the edge of Eliza's bed, stretching her legs out so as not to crumple the delicate light blue dress she was wearing for the music recital that evening.

Eliza turned away from the mirror, knowing the front few strands of her hair would never sit the way she wished they would despite hours of trying to curl them.

'He was a little scandalised I actually had the audacity to visit him at home, but once he had recovered from that he was perfectly pleasant.'

'Perfectly pleasant,' Lucy murmured. 'Why does that sound like an insult?'

Eliza sighed. She couldn't work out what it was about Lord Thannock that unsettled her so much. Perhaps it was the fact that she was already indebted to him and she didn't like the idea of someone else being in control of her fate.

'I don't understand why he is helping me. It is a great inconvenience to him and he doesn't get anything out of it.'

'From what Lady Mountjoy says he is a very kind and generous man.'

Eliza narrowed her eyes. In her experience everyone had an agenda. Everyone had a reason for offering favours, big or small. Even Lady Mountjoy was quite open that one of the reasons she had been so generous in bringing Eliza and the other three debutantes to London was because she loved the excitement and energy of a Season when there was matchmaking afoot.

'No one is that kind.'

'Maybe he is interested in getting to know you more?'

Eliza snorted. 'Hardly. I could believe it was Lady Mountjoy's intention to try to pair us off, to use the situation to encourage us together, but I can't believe Lord Thannock is interested in me.'

'Why not?'

'I spent the morning with him, Lucy. He was polite, civil, kind even, but he didn't really want to be there.'

'I'm sure you'll get to know him well over the coming few weeks.'

Eliza nodded, consciously having to relax the muscles in her face to stop herself from frowning. The last thing she wanted was to develop wrinkles between her brows before the age of twenty-two.

'I know I sound ungrateful, Lucy,' she said, flopping down beside her friend. 'In truth, I should be on my knees with gratitude that Lord Thannock has agreed to this and I'm not being sent home to Somerset in disgrace.'

'But you're not?'

Eliza was trying to formulate her answer, trying to

put into words the deep yearning she had for freedom, for a different type of future. It wasn't that she didn't wish to get married and settle down one day, more that if she did decide that was the right path for her she wanted it to be on her terms.

Before she could answer there was a knock on the door and Lady Mountjoy swept into the room.

'You both look beautiful,' she said as she ran her eyes over them. 'Are you ready for the evening?'

'I'm so eager to hear Mr Ramioli play,' Lucy said, her eyes shining with excitement.

'And how do you feel, Eliza?'

'A little nervous. I hope everything goes to plan.'

'It will, my dear, it is the perfect event to have your first appearance with Lord Thannock. I think this evening is going to be a success.'

Eliza nodded, feeling the little knot of nerves building in the pit of her stomach. She might not want to jump at the first proposal or suitable gentleman who came her way, but she was very aware she needed people to believe hers and Lord Thannock's subterfuge this evening or she would be cast out of society in disgrace before she had properly even entered it.

'I hope so.'

The next ten minutes were a flurry of activity as Lady Mountjoy tried to usher the four young ladies in her care out of the door of the town house and down to the awaiting carriage. As they clambered inside Eliza was surprised to find Lord Mountjoy already sitting there, a book in his hand and a contented smile on his face as his wife sat down next to him. Not once had he chivvied her along, instead content to quietly wait in the carriage until she was ready.

Eliza wasn't sure if she imagined the hush that fell over the room as she entered. Ideally she would like to be walking in on Lord Thannock's arm, but he'd argued people would be less inclined to gossip if they broke no more rules of society. So here she was, gripping Lucy's arm so tightly she worried she might leave a bruise.

'Everyone is staring at you,' Miss Huntley said, a little smirk on her face. 'Perhaps you should have stayed hidden in your bedroom.'

'Maybe they're staring at you. You have a little something on your face.' She couldn't help baiting Miss Huntley when she was around her—there was something entirely unpleasant about the young woman.

Lucy pulled her away before she and Miss Huntley could exchange any more sharp words and they made their way to the seats set out in front of a performance area.

It felt as though she were walking through a courtroom, ready to be judged by a jury of the *ton* and found wanting. She was grateful for Lucy's steady presence beside her, controlling the pace they walked at and smiling in greeting to the people they had been introduced to before. Jane also walked with them, motioning to a line of chairs that would seat them all and leave a spot on the end for Lord Thannock when he made his appearance.

'Is everyone staring?'

She saw Jane and Lucy exchange a glance before

they both vehemently shook their heads. 'Not at all,' Jane said quickly.

'You're kind, Jane, but you're a terrible liar.'

'They won't be staring in a minute. They'll forget all about you.'

It took all of Eliza's iron will not to turn around every few seconds to check whether Lord Thannock had arrived yet.

Around them people started to take their seats and their hostess for the evening, a rotund woman with rosy cheeks and a beaming smile, clapped her hands for her guests' attention.

Eliza felt like sinking lower into her chair. He wasn't going to come. All of this effort and she'd actually made it worse. She felt the sting in her eyes and quickly blinked, refusing to shed tears over this man. No one knew she was sitting here, further humiliated, no one except the Mountjoys and Lucy, Jane and Miss Huntley.

With a start she flicked a glance at Miss Huntley, but the young woman was sitting in her seat serenely as if she didn't care what was happening at the other end of the row.

'Dear friends, thank you so much for coming this evening,' Mrs Whitlaw said at the front of the room. 'I have such a treat in store for you I can hardly contain my excitement. I first heard Mr Ramioli play some years ago while honeymooning with my husband in Italy. I knew then he was something special and in the interceding years he has proved to be so much more than that.' She smiled and clapped her hands again. 'It is my delight to introduce Mr Ramioli.'

A short man with a shock of black hair and a thick moustache stepped into the room to a round of polite applause. At the same moment Eliza caught movement out of the corner of her eye and turned to see Lord Thannock slipping into the seat next to her.

'Good evening,' he murmured.

Eliza didn't know whether to cheer in relief that he had actually come or to reprimand him for being late.

'Good evening,' she said neutrally.

'Thank you for saving me a seat,' he said, leaning in a little closer so no one else would be able to hear what they were saying.

'I wasn't sure you were going to make use of it.'

'I never back out of a promise, Miss Stanley.'

As his breath tickled her neck, a shiver ran through her body and she felt as though her senses were enhanced, her awareness of everything around her heightened.

'Ready to make everyone believe we're madly in love?'

Her lips were suddenly dry and she could only croak out a quiet reply. Ignoring what the musician was saying at the front of the room, she half turned to face Lord Thannock, sucking in a breath of air when she saw him. He looked devastatingly handsome this evening. No wonder he was declared the most eligible bachelor in London. When making no effort he was attractive, but tonight, with his crisp white shirt and close-fitting jacket, his hair combed back and his eyes glittering in the candlelight, he would turn every head in the room.

She felt a heat deep inside her and frowned, making

an effort to ignore it. This response was not helpful. The last thing she needed was to develop an infatuation with the man sitting next to her. They needed to be logical, clear headed, and her being distracted by his dark eyes and alluring smile wouldn't help.

'Without further ado I will take my place,' Mr Ramioli said, sitting at the grand piano at the front of the room.

Eliza was glad of the distraction. Even she could tell Mr Ramioli was a talented pianist and soon everyone was engrossed in the performance.

'I suppose I should be murmuring sweet nothings in your ear,' Lord Thannock whispered as the music swelled.

'I suppose you should,' Eliza said with more composure than she felt, 'although no one can hear so you could say anything.'

'Anything?' Lord Thannock mused.

'Anything tedious,' Eliza corrected quickly. She wasn't sure if she would be able to maintain her cool demeanour if he started talking about anything intimate. Feeling the heat creep to her cheeks, she knew it was ridiculous to think he would lean in close and whisper something intimate in her ear when they were sitting in a crowded room of people.

'Something tedious…' He moved away for a second and Eliza desperately tried to slow her breathing. She wasn't sure why she was reacting like this to Lord Thannock of all people, but it needed to stop. 'I could list my favourite jams. Or tell you the names of all the dogs we owned when I was a child. There were a lot.'

Eliza made a slightly strangled noise, which he must have taken for acquiescence.

'Of course no one can argue that strawberry is king of the jams,' he said, the words murmured so quietly Eliza involuntarily leaned in a little closer to hear. 'Closely followed by raspberry. I am partial to a plum jam which is a controversial third choice, but I don't hold a high opinion of marmalade.'

The skin of her neck felt as though it was on fire and she had this momentary fantasy of him leaning in even closer, his lips almost on her skin.

She coughed and shifted in her seat.

'Are you blushing, Miss Stanley?'

'Talk of jams wouldn't make me blush,' she muttered curtly and then signalled they should focus on the music.

For the next twenty minutes Mr Ramioli impressed the audience with his skill on the piano, playing a variety of pieces to suit all tastes. Everyone was enraptured—everyone except Eliza. She was sitting completely still, pretending to be engrossed in the music, but instead she was trying to understand her reaction to the perfectly normal man sitting beside her.

Every other time they had met she hadn't felt like this and it wasn't as though he had changed who he was. A smart jacket and a crisp shirt didn't change the essence of a man and she had judged him to be a little too dull for her.

Eliza knew it was one of her faults, being quick to judge, but she found first impressions were rarely

wrong. Rarely didn't mean never, though. Perhaps Lord
Thannock was the one man in a hundred she had mis-
judged.

'You look very elegant tonight, Miss Stanley,' Lord
Thannock said as the pianist struck the last chord and
the assembled guests broke into a hearty applause.

'Thank you.' Eliza had chosen her attire carefully,
selecting a brilliant white dress with a pale pink satin
sash that sat under her bust. It was simple but well made
and she hoped it would conjure images of purity and in-
nocence in people's minds. A friend had once told her
a woman needed to use every weapon in her arsenal to
persuade people of her character and Eliza was determined not to miss a trick.

'Lord Thannock, how pleased we are you could join
us,' Lady Mountjoy said, a beaming smile on her face.
She gave a not-too-subtle wink to show she was about to
begin the subterfuge, and Eliza felt like rolling her eyes.
'Have you announced the news officially?' she asked
loudly, ensuring every curious ear nearby was listening.

'I have spoken to Miss Stanley's father,' Lord Thannock said, and Eliza was surprised to hear the lie slip off
his tongue so easily. For some reason she had assumed
he would find it difficult to engage in the subterfuge.
He seemed too honest, too invested in his morals. Something else she had got wrong about him. 'Our families
are aware of our intentions.'

'Do I understand congratulations are in order?' Mrs
Whitlaw, their hostess for the evening, swept in, her
eyes gleaming in delight. Eliza imagined it was a coup

to have her event as the place the most eligible bachelor in London's engagement was announced.

'Yes, Mrs Whitlaw,' Lord Thannock said, smiling down at Eliza with what appeared to be true affection in his eyes. 'Miss Stanley has accepted my proposal. We are engaged.'

'Oh, what fantastic news. Mrs Henlow, have you heard this?'

Watching in amazement at the speed the news spread across the drawing room, Eliza shook her head in disbelief.

'That's the first step complete,' Lord Thannock murmured in her ear. 'Now we have to persuade everyone I'm completely besotted with you.'

'And I with you?'

'Better feign mild uninterest if you plan on throwing me over for another man in a few weeks.'

'So I've enraptured you?'

'And you are doing your duty marrying a wealthy and titled gentleman, but when your true love appears you owe it to your heart to move on.'

Eliza wasn't sure about the last part, but she nodded anyway.

'Don't they look so in love,' Mrs Whitlaw was saying to Lady Mountjoy.

Making the mistake of glancing up at the Viscount, Eliza felt her breath catch in her chest. He really was a good actor—for an instant even she had believed his affection for her.

Chapter Five

Sam settled back into his seat as the pianist played a lively piece in the second half of his set. There was no denying the man was talented and all in all he was enjoying his evening much more than he'd thought he would. Before leaving the house tonight he would have been able to list two dozen things he would rather be doing with his time, but here he was, quite contented with how the evening was turning out.

He glanced at the young woman beside him. Her eyes were fixed on the pianist at the front of the room and her lips were ever so slightly parted. They looked velvety and smooth and he had the absurd urge to lean over in his seat and brush a kiss against them.

Sitting up a little straighter, he surreptitiously pinched the palm of his hand, trying to knock a little sense into himself. Miss Stanley was *not* the sort of young woman he would ever allow himself to fall for. He was sure she was pleasant enough, and he would not wish any ill on her, but she was exactly what he had always promised himself he would avoid.

She had that same dangerous streak, the same desire to socialise and surround herself with the superficial that he saw in his mother, the characteristics that had ultimately driven his father to an early grave.

He would do his good deed, ensuring Miss Stanley's reputation was not entirely ruined by her foolishness, and then he would retreat to the country and forget she ever existed.

Next to him Miss Stanley shifted and then leaned her head in towards his. 'I think our ruse may be working.'

'Oh?'

'A few young women have given me jealous looks, but the older people among the guests are looking at us with indulgence.'

'As if they will pardon our foolishness.'

'Exactly.'

He watched as she straightened in her chair with a relieved smile on her face. For a few minutes the music swelled and within ten Mr Ramioli had finished and was standing to take a bow.

'Thank you, Mr Ramioli, I am sure everyone here will agree that was the most wonderful thing we've ever heard,' Mrs Whitlaw said, the words gushing out as if she struggled to contain them. Mr Ramioli took a bow, one hand resting casually on the top of the piano.

'If you would all care to move through the door to your left, there are refreshments in the next room.'

'Do you play, Miss Stanley?'

Eliza let out a laugh and then shook her head. 'No.'

'What is so funny?'

She looked up at him for a moment as if deciding

whether to let him in on a secret and then took his arm
and moved in closer so only he could hear.

'It was a great subject of contention in my house. My
mother was keen for my younger sister and I to learn the
piano, she thought it would help us to marry well. My
father told her he wasn't wasting money on teaching us
to play just to land us husbands. He wanted to focus any
little spare money they had on educating my brother.'

'Ah.'

'My mother could play, but we didn't have access
to a piano so we could not even learn from her.' Miss
Stanley shook her head and a smile spread across her
lips. 'When I learned I was going to be joining Lady
Mountjoy for the Season I panicked, knowing she would
expect a young lady to be able to play the piano and
paint with watercolours and probably even speak a little French.'

'Lady Mountjoy would not hold it against you if you
could not do any of those things.'

'I know that now,' Miss Stanley said and he could see
she had to stop herself from rolling her eyes. 'But I didn't
then and I was so desperate to get away from Somerset
that I didn't want anything to jeopardise my chances.'

'What did you do?'

'I paid a girl from the village to teach me one piece
and then paid her more to give me the key to her house
so I could sneak in when everyone was at church to
practice. I played it again and again and again until
every note was perfect.'

'Please tell me you've had to use it, that all that effort was not in vain.'

Miss Stanley smiled, and Sam felt as though he were being pulled into her secret world where only the two of them existed.

'In the first couple of days at Lady Mountjoy's house she asked us all to play for her. Miss Huntley is incredible on the piano, by the way, if you're looking for a musical prodigy and can withstand her snide comments. I waited until last and played my tune perfectly, politely declined to play another and stepped away from the piano with grace and no one knows I can't play anything more than one song.'

He smiled wryly. 'It was worth paying for the lesson, then?'

'Yes, although the deception does mean I live in fear any time I see a piano in the room.'

They followed Lady Mountjoy and the rest of Miss Stanley's companions through to the dining room where drinks and light refreshments were laid out on the long dining table and little groups had begun to form. Mrs Whitlaw was flitting among her guests, introducing Mr Ramioli who was smiling politely but looked as though he would rather be elsewhere.

'I hear congratulations are in order,' a strikingly beautiful young woman said as they found a spot to stand in among the crowd. She looked at Miss Stanley expectantly, waiting to be introduced.

'Lord Thannock, this is Miss Huntley. Miss Huntley, this is Lord Thannock.'

He could feel the tension in Miss Stanley as she introduced the other young woman and wondered what was at the root of the obvious dislike between them.

'You are a generous man, Lord Thannock,' Miss Huntley said, fixing him with a dazzling smile. 'Little Eliza must be so grateful.'

'You know of the circumstances?' he said in a hushed voice. He wasn't aware that anyone except he, Miss Stanley and Lady Mountjoy knew of their deception.

'She listened at the door when we were talking with Lady Mountjoy.'

Miss Huntley gave a slightly too-loud laugh. 'You jest, Miss Stanley. I was merely admiring the paintings in the hall and happened to overhear you talking. There was nothing planned or malicious about it.'

Sam shifted uncomfortably. The more people who knew of their deception the more it was likely to go wrong.

'Of course I will not mention your little arrangement to anyone else,' Miss Huntley said with a subtle flutter of her eyelashes.

'Thank you, Miss Stanley and I would be most grateful.'

'Perhaps in turn you might do me a favour?'

Resisting the urge to raise an eyebrow, he inclined his head, indicating she should go on.

'Perhaps you might introduce me to a few of your friends. I am eager to make the acquaintance of as many people as possible this Season, as I will likely only have the one.'

'That does not seem unreasonable, Miss Huntley. I will be sure to do so when the opportunity arises.'

Miss Huntley gave a curtsy and with a beaming smile sailed away.

'Isn't she vile?' Miss Stanley whispered.

'Vile?'

'Don't tell me you were as taken in by her superficial charm as every other gentleman we meet.'

'You really don't like her, do you?'

'I don't like people who act in one way to people they don't see as important and another way to people who might be useful to them.'

Sam considered Miss Stanley for a moment. 'You are right about that. My father always used to say you can tell the character of a man by how he treats those below him on the social ladder.'

'He sounds like a wise man.'

'In many ways he was.'

'But not in all?'

Sam shook his head, knowing Miss Stanley was the wrong person to discuss this with. He had idolised his father when he was young, loved the kind and gentle man more than anyone else in the world, but in those years between childhood and adulthood he had sometimes felt some of that respect slipping away as he wondered why his father put up with so much from his mother. If he was honest, it had stung that his father had always chosen his mother or his work over Sam, but he hardly liked to admit that to himself let alone anyone else.

'My parents' marriage…' he said and trailed off.

Miss Stanley must have seen the reluctance in his eyes to discuss his parents and he was grateful when she nodded briefly as if he had said enough on the matter and moved on.

'What are our plans for tomorrow, now the engagement has been announced?'

'I am busy tomorrow evening,' he said quickly, 'but perhaps we could meet for a ride in Hyde Park.' He frowned before adding quickly, 'You do know how to ride?'

'I may not be a talented musician but I can ride, Lord Thannock.'

'Good. That is settled then. I will bring the horses.'

Chapter Six

'I have been congratulated no less than six times already on my matchmaking prowess,' Lady Mountjoy said as she walked arm in arm with Eliza along the pavement, heading towards Hyde Park. It was a cold, crisp day, with some of the leaves lying on the ground still white from the frost even though it was past noon. 'Your first week into your debut in London and you've captured the heart of London's most eligible bachelor.'

'I wish people would be less interested,' Eliza said, wiggling her fingers inside her gloves to try to keep them warm. 'It is going to make it much harder to quietly drift apart if everyone is so invested in our relationship.'

Lady Mountjoy waved a hand dismissively in the air. 'These things have a way of working themselves out.'

Eliza pressed her lips together, wondering if the older woman was hoping the forced proximity over the next few weeks would bring Eliza and Lord Thannock closer in more ways than one and they would decide to make the engagement a true one. She nearly laughed out loud at the idea.

'How do you know Lord Thannock?' she asked instead, remembering the fondness in Lady Mountjoy's eyes when she spoke to the Viscount.

'Lord Thannock is friends with my son, Tom. They are of an age and met at school. Lord Thannock spent many a happy summer holiday running wild around our estate with Tom and the rest of my darling children. It was good for him.'

'Because he was an only child.'

'Yes. He lived in a big old country house and often in the holidays he would be all alone. His father was very involved in Parliament and his charity work in London so would be away much of the time and his mother...' Lady Mountjoy trailed off. 'Well, she wasn't there that much either. It is no life for a child to be raised by servants.'

'He seems very fond of you.'

'He is very good and very sweet, although he tries to hide it behind that gruff facade to the rest of society.'

'To keep all the ambitious debutantes away?'

'Yes. He hated being dubbed London's most eligible bachelor—said it attracted the wrong sort of woman, not the sort he would ever consider settling down with.'

Eliza fell silent, wondering what sort that would be. Perhaps someone good and kind and gentle like Lucy.

'I'm sorry I've made such a mess of our first few weeks in London,' Eliza said as they went through the ornate gates at the entrance to the park.

'Can I let you into a little secret?' Lady Mountjoy

lowered her voice and bent her head in a conspiratorial manner. 'I've found it all rather thrilling. *This* is what I remember the Season to be like, little dramas and challenges and keeping your fingers crossed that everything turns out well in the end.' She patted Eliza on the hand. 'I know it is your life, my dear, and your future. I don't want you to think that I am finding fun in something that may have lasting consequences for you, but I do want you to know that I will do everything in my not insignificant power to make sure you end up happy at the close of the Season.'

Eliza gripped the older woman's hand and squeezed. 'Thank you, that is very kind of you.'

'I see Lord Thannock. Doesn't he cut a fine figure on horseback?' Lady Mountjoy said with a beaming smile, and Eliza couldn't even manage to roll her eyes at the older woman.

'Good morning, Miss Stanley, Lady Mountjoy,' Lord Thannock said and he dismounted, holding both horses' reins in one hand. 'Isn't it a fine day for a ride?'

'You seem in good spirits this morning, Sam dear,' Lady Mountjoy said.

'I am. I've had some good news.'

'I am pleased for you.'

'What will you do while we ride?' Eliza turned to the older woman with a frown.

'Don't you worry about me, my dear, I have arranged to meet a friend in the coffee house at the edge of the park. Shall I see you back here in one hour?'

'Thank you,' Eliza said.

'Will you permit me to assist you in mounting?' Lord Thannock said as Lady Mountjoy left them.

Nodding, Eliza walked round to the front of her horse. She loved the excitement and noise of the city, but she had been raised a country girl and had learned to ride almost as soon as she could walk. Gently, she stroked the horse on the nose and murmured a greeting, before coming round to the saddle.

She eyed it nervously. At home they did have a side saddle, but she normally either rode bareback or just with a normal saddle, her skirts hitched up to her knees. There had been no money for a riding habit when she was learning to ride so it felt constrictive around her legs and, even though she was normally confident on horseback, she had the horrible notion that her feet would get caught in the material of her habit and she would fly from the horse and land in a tangled mess.

'Ready?'

'Yes.'

Lord Thannock stood behind her and held out his hands, ready to boost her up into the saddle. Eliza took a deep breath and shook off her worries. Riding was something she was good at. A different type of dress and an uncomfortable saddle didn't change her skill as a horsewoman.

She pulled herself up easily and settled in the saddle. Below her, Lord Thannock waited patiently until she was comfortable to hand her the reins. She watched as he effortlessly swung up on to the back of his horse and then turned to her.

'Shall we?'

They settled into a gentle pace, setting off first down the path and then on to the grass to allow the horses a little more space. Lord Thannock seemed to know where he was going so Eliza allowed herself to sit back and enjoy the ride.

'What is your good news, Lord Thannock?' Eliza asked after a few minutes of riding in silence.

'Perhaps you should call me Sam when it is just the two of us,' he said, smiling over at her. 'Lord Thannock sounds so formal when we are meant to be besotted with each other.'

'I suppose we are going to be spending a lot of time together. You will call me Eliza?'

'If you agree.'

She thought about it for a moment and then nodded. 'I think it is a good idea. So what is your good news, Sam?'

'You will think me a terrible person if I tell you.'

Eliza laughed. 'Lady Mountjoy is sure you're a saint. I hardly think you could do *anything* terrible.'

'My mother has plans to leave London next week.' He waited for a moment, then shook his head. 'I told you it is terrible to be so happy about a family member leaving.'

'Not terrible,' Eliza said with a shake of her head. 'Not if she causes you distress.'

'I cannot claim distress, mild inconvenience at the worst.'

'What is it about her that unsettles you so much?'

He paused for a long moment, looking out into the distance. 'I suppose it is never knowing what she is going to do next. The woman is so unpredictable and I do not like things that are not ordered and done right.'

'I admit I do not know her, but she sounds as though she might be fun,' Eliza said, knowing this could be the wrong thing to say.

'Oh, she is fun, without a doubt. If you want someone to be the life and soul of an event, then invite my mother. She will have everyone dancing and laughing and having a merry time.'

'But not so much at home?'

'She saves the best of herself for everyone else.' He shrugged. 'Let's not talk about her. I am glad she has plans to go and stay with a friend in Scotland for a few months. She will be happy and I will be happy and that is enough.'

Eliza wondered whether she might get to meet Sam's mother before she left for her trip. She felt as though it would be interesting to see such a part of Sam's life, but acknowledged it was none of her business given that she was only going to be linked to him for a short time.

'We should head for the busier areas of the park,' Sam said, turning his horse's head gently. 'That way we will be seen by more people.'

'You have a very strategic approach to this.'

'I have always thought it is best to have a plan for every contingency, then you will never be caught out.' He looked at her with a half-smile. 'I assume you are the opposite—you'd rather not plan anything and enjoy the spontaneous.'

'There is something wonderful about not knowing what is going to happen next. I love the thrill of the unknown.' She grimaced as she continued, 'That was one of the reasons I was so keen to get out of Somerset for even a short while. Everything was so familiar, so routine. Each day was exactly like the one before it, there was no variation, no excitement. I could see my whole life stretching out ahead of me, talking to the same people, going on the same walks, doing the same things.'

'What is it you want from life, aside from not what you had in Somerset?'

Eliza took a moment to think. She'd been asking herself this these last few days. For so long she had been focused on getting away from her old life that she hadn't considered what it was she wanted from her new one. It wasn't even about climbing the social ladder, marrying someone rich and titled. She'd had an informal offer from a wealthy older gentleman in Somerset, a friend of her father's. If she had wanted a comfortable, quiet country life with someone affable, then she would have accepted that.

She knew one day she probably would have to marry—that was the way of the world. A young woman couldn't prosper and thrive on her own unless she had some sort of extraordinary talent.

'I don't know what I want, but I feel as though for twenty-one years I've lived in this little bubble of an existence, mixing with the same people who do the same things. I want to see some of the world, meet different people, and then perhaps I will know what I want to do. Does that sound silly?'

'Not at all. How can you be expected to know what you want when you haven't experienced much?'

'Every new experience gives me such a thrill. I can't

see how settling down to a life of running a household could ever compare.'

'Perhaps you will feel differently when you fall in love.'

Eliza screwed up her face. It wasn't that she didn't believe in love—her parents were a good example of a gentle, unobtrusive love that engulfed everyone around them—it was more that she couldn't imagine ever falling in love with anyone enough to want to settle down with them.

'Not every marriage has to be one of dull domesticity,' Sam said with an amused smile. 'You might fall in love with an army captain and follow him across Europe. Or you might marry a man who becomes ambassador to India.'

Eliza nodded thoughtfully. 'That would be more exciting that becoming Mrs Bernard Newbury of Lowton, Somerset...' She paused, wondering how to get across how unsatisfactory that all felt. 'It would still be following a husband's lead, though, wouldn't it? I feel as though I want something of my own, something I choose to do.' She shook her head and laughed. 'I am being both far too vague and very specific in one sentence. In truth, I do not know what I want, but it isn't the life that was planned out for me in Somerset.'

'Maybe you need a cause.'

'A cause?'

'Yes, a project, something that you care about, that you want to devote your time and your energy to.'

'As interesting as that sounds, I fear you need to be wealthy to have a cause.'

'Not everything is measured in monetary value.'

'No, but to have the time to devote to a cause, the funds to support yourself while doing whatever it is that needs to be done…'

'You may be right,' Sam conceded, then brightened. 'Then maybe in a suitor you are looking for someone wealthy who will give you your freedom to pursue your passions as you wish.'

'Do you know anyone like that?'

'Good Lord, no, I doubt that sort of man exists, but we can add it to your list of desires.'

'Has Lady Mountjoy been giving you a lesson on how to matchmake?'

Sam laughed at this, throwing his head back and letting out the first proper laugh she had heard from him. He looked younger when he was laughing, as if the cares of the world had slipped from his shoulders and he was just a man having a good time. Eliza felt her breath catch in her throat. She wanted him to look at her, to lean closer and murmur something that was private to them and include her in his laughter.

Quickly, she pushed the thought away—all she should want from Lord Thannock was exactly what he was giving her: a fake engagement for a few weeks.

They had reached a busier area of the park and were riding side by side along one of the wide gravel paths. Other riders were doing the same alongside some carriages driving slowly up and down. It was a cold afternoon, but it hadn't deterred people from promenading or riding, wrapped up in their winter coats and furs.

'Good afternoon, Lord Thannock, Miss Stanley,' a portly older gentleman said as they passed him riding in the opposite direction with a younger man who looked to be his son.

'Good afternoon.'

'Who was that?' Eliza spoke quietly once the man had moved away. 'I'm sure I've never met him before, so how does he know who I am?'

'You're notorious.'

'Notorious doesn't sound good.'

'Perhaps notorious is too strong a word. You're well known in our social circle. There will not be a household that has not discussed your predicament.'

Eliza closed her eyes for a moment and wondered if Somerset was far enough away to be spared from the scandal. It would horrify her parents to know she was being talked about like this and she couldn't bear them being disappointed in her.

'It will settle down. Everything is fresh and new, remember. In a few weeks people won't have forgotten exactly, but it will not be so interesting to them.'

Nodding, Eliza wondered if it was true. Everyone kept promising the scandal would die down soon, but what if they were wrong?

'I wonder...' she said, but stopped as she noticed Sam was frowning into the distance, not paying her any attention at all. Without any explanation, he slipped from the back of his horse and thrust the reins in her direction.

'Hold these,' he said, his eyes still fixed on something Eliza couldn't make out.

'Sam,' she said quietly, and as he stepped away,

called out, 'Lord Thannock,' a little louder, but he was too preoccupied to notice.

All she could do was watch as he strode across the gravel path, not noticing the people he passed on the way who had to swerve to avoid a collision. He reached a group of three women, one older and two younger, probably a mother and two daughters by the way they were walking close together. At first Eliza thought Sam must be heading for them and wondered what the three inoffensive-looking women had done to inspire so much ire. Then she watched as he continued around the far side of the little group and grabbed a small child by the jacket.

The three women exclaimed in surprise and Eliza knew she had to get closer to find out what was happening. Carefully, she dismounted and led both horses nearer to the little group, stopping when she was close enough to hear, but still far enough away to remain inconspicuous.

'I am sorry to have startled you,' he said to the three ladies, holding the struggling young boy with ease by the collar of his shirt. 'I think there has been a misunderstanding. I saw you drop your coin purse, Miss Amelia, and this young lad was just about to return it to you.'

Eliza started in amazement as the young boy stopped wriggling and looked up at Sam, screwing up his face into an expression of annoyance.

'Dropped my coin purse?' one of the tall young ladies said, her hand flying to her chest.

'It is easy to do,' Sam said quickly and gave the boy a gentle shake. 'Hand it over.'

Reluctantly, the boy thrust a hand into his pocket and pulled out an embroidered velvet purse. He weighed it in his palm for a moment and then held it out.

'You dropped this, miss,' he said, chancing a smile.

'Oh.' Miss Amelia took the purse and then looked to her mother for guidance.

'Should we take him to the magistrate, Lord Thannock?'

Immediately, the boy started wriggling again and pulling at his collar to get away.

'No need, Mrs Appleby. I will let you ladies continue with your walk this fine day. I shall deal with the boy.'

'That is most kind of you, Lord Thannock. Thank you for coming to our rescue.'

As the three women moved away, Eliza approached the spot where Sam was left holding the young boy by the collar.

'What are you doing out here?' Sam said softly to the boy. 'Shouldn't you be in your lessons?'

'The new teacher caned my hands for...' he paused, screwing up his face as he searched for the word '...insubordination. I can't hold a pencil so how am I supposed to write anything?'

Sam let go of the boy's collar and inspected his hands, a furrow appearing on his brow as he spotted the raised wheals. Eliza expected the lad to run as soon as he was let go, but instead he seemed happy to stand and show Sam his hands.

'He's a monster, cruel, all the boys say so.'

'I will talk to Miss Hardman about the teacher,' Sam

said, dropping the boy's hands, 'but it is not an excuse for you to be out here picking pockets.'

'I know.'

'If someone else had caught you there would be no second chances, Bertie.'

'I know. Are you going to tell Miss Hardman?'

There was a long pause before Sam answered. 'No, but I will come by in the next few days to speak to her. I don't want to hear you've got in any trouble between now and then.'

'I'll be on my best behaviour.'

'Good. Now go straight home, no dawdling.'

The young boy saluted and then ran off through the park, disappearing in among the crowds.

Eliza was baffled by the whole thing. She didn't see what connection Sam could have with the scruffy young boy who seemed to hold him in high regard.

'I apologise,' Sam said as he took the reins of the horse from her.

'What just happened?'

'I know that boy from an orphanage I donate to. I saw him slipping the coin purse from Miss Amelia Appleby and couldn't stand by without intervening.'

'How on earth did you see it happen?'

Sam grimaced. 'I saw Bertie first and there is no good reason for him to be sneaking through the crowds in the park at this time in the afternoon. I was watching him when he dipped his hand in to take the coin purse.'

Eliza had so many questions she barely knew where to start. 'He seemed to know you well.'

Shrugging, Sam began to lead his horse down the

path and Eliza fell into step beside him. 'I drop in to visit sometimes and have spent a little time with the children. Bertie has been at the orphanage for a couple of years, but his circumstances were dire before that. He lived on the streets for six months after his mother died and learned all the tricks he needed to keep himself alive.'

'You really are too good to be true, aren't you?' Eliza murmured. She doubted many people knew of Sam's good deeds and it wouldn't have made him seem more eligible or desirable to the young ladies of the *ton*, but it was another thing about him that made him a good person.

'Come on,' Sam said, checking his pocket watch. 'Lady Mountjoy will be waiting for us.

Eliza caught up and side by side they walked back through Hyde Park to their rendezvous point.

Chapter Seven

'Please do not feel the need to accompany me, Mother, I am sure there are a hundred things you'd rather be doing tonight.'

'Nonsense, darling. My Samuel is engaged and I haven't yet met your fiancée. That is reason enough. Besides, I haven't been to a London ball this Season and it is time I remedied that.'

Sam straightened his cravat in the mirror and tried to fix his face into a neutral expression. He found his mother a difficult woman to read and he wasn't sure how much of his exasperation she'd picked up on. Part of him thought she couldn't have sailed through life as oblivious as she often made out.

'How do I look?'

'Very nice as always, Mother. Are you ready?'

The carriage ride was short and Sam was glad when they stepped out into the cool night air.

'I will be leaving after an hour or two, but I have no objection to you staying longer. I can walk home and you can take the carriage when you are ready,' Sam said as he offered his mother his arm.

'You'll only stay an hour? How funny you are, Samuel. This is a ball, not a funeral. It gets better as the night goes on.'

Sam fixed a smile on his lips as they greeted their hostess and debated if he would rather keep his mother close so he could keep an eye on her antics or escape to a quiet corner as soon as possible.

'Where is this fiancée of yours, then?' his mother whispered as they entered the ballroom.

'Lady Thannock,' a familiar voice called out, and Sam felt the relief flood through him as Lady Mountjoy hurried over. 'How wonderful to see you. It has been too long. You are looking well.'

'You, too, Lady Mountjoy.'

'I didn't realise you were going to be in attendance tonight,' Lady Mountjoy said, flicking a look of concern at Sam.

Lady Thannock lowered her head so she could drop her voice, but still be heard by Lady Mountjoy. 'I had to hear my son was engaged from someone else. I realised if I wanted to meet this young lady then I would have to step into his world.'

'This is your world as well, Mother,' Sam said, trying to relax his jaw. They had only been in the ballroom for a minute and already his whole face was aching.

'Let me find Miss Stanley and we can introduce you,' Lady Mountjoy said placatingly.

'Yes, good. And I will find a little glass of something.'

'I'll find Miss Stanley,' Sam said to Lady Mountjoy as his mother glided away. 'It is only fair I warn her first.'

'I will keep an eye on your mother.'

Sam paused and then on a whim reached out and took the older woman's hand and gave it a quick squeeze before turning on his heel and striding through the crowd. He spotted Eliza surrounded by a group of young gentlemen, all listening intently to what she had to say. As he neared, she laughed at something one of the men said and for a moment it made him pause. There was something so merry and carefree in that laugh that for an instant he wanted to push through the circle and ask her what had made her laugh so joyfully.

'Miss Stanley,' he said, noticing how the young gentlemen all took a step back as he approached.

'Lord Thannock, how lovely to see you this evening. Do you know Mr Roberts, Mr Tonington and Mr Hilway?'

'Good evening,' he said brusquely, turning his attention on the three young men for no more than half a second. 'Can I request the pleasure of your company for a few minutes, Miss Stanley?'

Eliza smiled and inclined her head, but the smile didn't quite reach her eyes. 'Of course, Lord Thannock. Gentlemen, it has been lovely talking to you, I do hope we get the opportunity to dance later.'

She placed a delicate hand on Sam's arm and allowed him to escort her away from the little group.

'What are you doing?' she muttered once they were far enough away not to be overheard.

'Claiming my fiancée for a few minutes.'

'How on earth am I meant to catch the attention of other eligible gentlemen if you whisk me away as soon as I start to talk to them?'

Sam glanced over his shoulder. 'Trust me, it won't hurt your chances. They are all following you with their eyes.'

'What is so important?'

'My mother is here.' He heard the growl in his voice and tried to let go of some of the tension he felt in his shoulders and jaw. It was no use. Every muscle was clenched in anticipation for what might come.

'Your mother,' Eliza said eagerly. 'How wonderful. I was hoping I might get to meet her.' Some of the happiness fled from her face when she saw Sam's expression. 'This isn't a good thing?' Then quickly she shook her head. 'Of course, you don't want to introduce me to her when you know in a few weeks I will no longer be in your life.'

'It's not that.'

Eliza leaned her head to one side and regarded him. 'She can't be as bad as all that.'

Sam closed his eyes for a moment and then summoned a smile. 'Hopefully not. Maybe I am overreacting. Come on, let's get this over with.'

'Darling Miss Stanley, how beautiful you are,' Lady Thannock said as she pulled Eliza into an embrace. 'Samuel, she is the most beautiful woman in the room, what good taste you have.'

'Quite,' Sam said, aware of the people around them looking on surreptitiously.

'You must tell me all about yourself.' He watched

as his mother linked arms with Eliza and pulled her to one side.

'Fortitude,' Lady Mountjoy whispered in his ear. 'She has only had one glass of champagne—I managed to signal the footman to pass us by.'

'Thank you, although I doubt it was her first of the evening.' His mother hadn't always been a drinker, but as the years had passed she had started to consume more and more alcohol. She often talked about the buzz of excitement she used to get when socialising as a young woman, never knowing who was going to ask her to dance, never knowing what the evening would bring. He often wondered if as the years passed the thrill had dulled a little and she had turned to alcohol and cards to get that same high.

'Tell me, Miss Stanley, how did you and my son meet?' Away from Lady Mountjoy and her son, Lady Thannock was a little less effusive and her words had a steely quality to them.

'We were introduced at a ball. I understand Lord Thannock knows Lady Mountjoy well and she is my sponsor for the Season.'

'Forgive me my questions, but I am a little confused about the timeline. You have been in London for just a few weeks, is that right?'

Eliza glanced over her shoulder, but saw Sam was not going to be able to come to her rescue. With a steadying breath she gave her most charming smile and nodded.

'And yet you had time to get to know my son, fall in love and decide you wanted to spend the rest of your lives together all before the ball where you were caught in a darkened room together?'

Eliza felt her mouth go dry. From how Sam had been portraying his mother she had imagined a less astute woman, someone who was too caught up in her own world to notice what was going on with anyone else. She was fast learning that wasn't the case with Lady Thannock.

Lady Thannock leaned in closer, and Eliza could smell the alcohol on her breath.

'I don't believe it,' she whispered in Eliza's ear. 'I don't believe a single word of it.'

'Lady Thannock—' Eliza said, but the older woman cut her off with a raised finger.

'I know all the little tricks a woman employs, Miss Stanley. I also know that my son is deemed the most eligible bachelor of the Season. I can see why you would seek to trap him and force him to marry you, he is one of the wealthiest, most influential men in London and you…' She gave Eliza a look that said more than words could. '*You* are a conniving little country girl who has seen an opportunity out of mediocrity.'

Eliza waited to check Lady Thannock had finally finished, then drew herself up to her full height. It was still a head and shoulders shorter than the woman in front of her, but Eliza had never suffered from a lack of confidence, so she began to speak quietly but firmly.

'I am sorry you think so poorly of me, but I am more sorry that you think so little of your son. Lord Thannock is a grown man, not only capable of making his own decisions, but clearly very successful at doing so.'

'Even the most astute of men can have their heads turned by a pretty girl.'

Eliza felt herself waver. It didn't feel right arguing with Sam's mother like this, especially when the older woman was right to doubt their relationship, but equally it wasn't her place to confide in Lady Thannock when her own son had decided not to.

She didn't know what else to say, but Lady Thannock was gripping her arm hard, not letting her escape back to the safety of Sam and Lady Mountjoy.

'My son may not confide in me, he may not even particularly trust me, but I know him, Miss Stanley, I know what is best for him…' she paused and said a little louder although Eliza doubted anyone else could hear over the hum of chatter in the room '…and you are not it.'

She let go of Eliza's arm with a flourish, and Eliza staggered back, thankful she was close to the wall or she would have tumbled for sure. Watching Lady Thannock glide off into the crowd, she felt stunned as if she couldn't quite believe what had just happened. Eliza was not one to panic, just as she wasn't one to cry, but right now she felt as if something was gripping her heart and squeezing and making it feel as though she couldn't get enough air to breathe.

With her head down, she walked briskly through the ballroom, making her way to the glass doors that led out on to a little terrace. It was a cold night and as the frosty air hit her she shivered, but didn't change her mind. In a way the coldness was refreshing, exactly what she needed to clear her head.

Looking up at the sky, she tried to focus on the few

stars she could see. At home in Somerset on a clear night you could see hundreds of stars, but here in the capital there never seemed to be so many visible. Still, there were a few twinkling in the sky and it felt good to focus on something that was so distant.

'It looked as though you and my mother were having a good talk.' She hadn't heard Sam slip out on to the terrace, but felt his presence as he came and stood beside her. Close, but not so close they were touching.

'We certainly talked, or at least your mother did. I wouldn't class it as *good*.'

Beside her, Sam let out a sigh and she saw him run a hand through his hair. 'I'm sorry.'

'It isn't your fault. We are not responsible for our relatives.'

'What did she say?'

'She doubted our story of falling in love and then planning on announcing the engagement the night we were caught at Lady Mountjoy's ball, and she questioned the timeline.'

'My mother always was sharp, even with a few drinks inside her.'

'Perhaps you should tell her the truth. Would she really object to you helping me out in this way?'

'She cannot keep a secret. Not when...' He trailed off and fell silent for a few moments before continuing, 'Not when she has been drinking.'

Eliza had known a woman who had drunk to excess back home. At first she was thought of as a fun guest to have around, but soon she was shunned for her behaviour. It had been uncomfortable for everyone involved.

Sam shook his head decisively. 'It is only a few more

days. She will leave for Scotland soon and before she returns we will have gone our separate ways.'

Opening her mouth to protest again, Eliza promptly shut it before she said anything. She had always been taught not to meddle in other people's family affairs. People didn't like their families to be criticised even if they were in the habit of doing it themselves.

'We should return to the ball before we create an even bigger scandal,' Eliza said, shivering in the cold.

'Are you enjoying it? Or rather were you enjoying it before my mother cornered you?'

'Yes. I love the dancing and meeting all these interesting people.'

'I'm sorry I took you away from your gaggle of suitors.'

'They were entertaining, although I'm not sure they had much substance.'

Sam held out his arm and together they walked back into the ballroom just as their hostess called for dancers for the next dance.

'Would you care to dance with me?'

Eliza gave him a dazzling smile and for an instant he couldn't focus on anything else but her lips. They were pink and rosy and looked ever so soft. He was so distracted that he didn't even hear her answer and had to assume by the fact she was still standing there in front of him she had agreed.

It felt as though she fitted perfectly in his arms as they took their places on the dance floor among the other couples for the waltz and Sam marvelled at how quickly Miss Eliza Stanley had started to get under his skin. Only a couple of weeks ago he wouldn't have recognised her name and now here he was actually enjoying a ball with her by his side.

She smiled up at him as they began to waltz and for a minute he allowed himself to be in the moment and enjoy the dance. He'd always been a good dancer, but over the years had avoided balls as much as possible so hadn't spent much time waltzing in the last decade. It surprised him to find that with Eliza in his arms it was an enjoyable experience.

'You look happy,' Eliza murmured up at him.

He adjusted his expression into a frown. 'Is that better? More natural?'

'Stop it, go back to smiling. It is nice to see you smile.'

'Everyone will think there is something wrong with me.'

'Everyone will think you're happy.'

He spun Eliza and brought her back to his body a little too sharpy, feeling her bump against him before she was able to right herself.

'You are a good dancer, Lord Thannock.'

'Thank you. You sound surprised.'

'There is a lot of talk about you among the debutantes.'

'Oh.'

'Apparently you don't dance much. Or smile much.'

'Yet here I am doing both.'

'*I* must be a good influence.' She grinned at him. 'They think you are mysterious and brooding, which is apparently a good thing.'

'Brooding,' he muttered, wondering whether it really was a good thing.

'And aloof.'

'Now I know that isn't a compliment.'

'Not for a woman, but I think it makes you even more attractive to these debutantes. They want to be the one who breaks down your barriers and reveals the sensitive and caring man underneath.'

Sam scoffed, but saw beneath the teasing Eliza was telling the truth. 'How do they feel about you being the one to *break down my barriers*?'

'Jealous, although none of them would admit it. I think there will be a lot of spiteful comments once we move on.'

For the first time since he had become embroiled in this pretence, Sam felt a pang of emotion that one day soon they would go their separate ways and most likely their paths would not cross again. Shaking himself, he searched for the voice of reason. Pretending to be engaged to Eliza wasn't the terrible burden he had thought it might be, but only because it wasn't a real engagement. He wouldn't be feeling this way if he was looking at his whole life being tied to her.

As the music swelled and then faded away he looked into Eliza's eyes and felt a surge of desire, stepping away quickly to suppress it.

'Your suitors are waiting,' he said gruffly and led her to the edge of the dance floor and walked away without a backward glance.

Chapter Eight

'I do not want to interfere.' Lady Mountjoy's voice came from behind him, and even though he knew the next words would be interfering he couldn't help but smile. The older woman had a special place in his affections after the many summers he had spent at her country estate running wild with her children.

'Surely you wouldn't interfere,' he said with a smile, standing as she swept into the room and took the seat opposite him.

'Don't tease, Sam. I know what I am, but all I can say is my intentions are always good.'

'Of that I have no doubt.'

'I saw you stalk off after your waltz with Miss Stanley.'

'We had finished our dance.'

'Pish posh. There was more to it than that.'

Sam eyed the older woman intently, wondering what her motivation was for seeking him out here in a quiet corner of the house. He had escaped the ball for a few minutes, trying doors off the hallway until he had found his way into a quiet little room he thought was probably used as a private sitting room. For a moment he had hesitated, remembering what had happened the last time he'd gone into a darkened room at a ball, but the allure of a little peace had been too much.

'Did you know I am about to become a grandmother?' Lady Mountjoy smiled, a big beaming smile. 'Tom's dear wife, Rebecca, is about five months pregnant.'

'That is wonderful news. I must write to congratulate them.'

'Tom and Rebecca are very happy. Their marriage is a good one, I think.'

'He's a lucky man.'

'Yes, he is. All my children have been lucky in marriage.'

Sam suppressed a smile. He knew where this conversation was headed, but was happy to let it play out how Lady Mountjoy had planned.

'I had a hand in arranging all of their matches—not directly of course, I would never presume to tell anyone who to marry, but with an introduction here and a nudge there…'

'I'm sure all your children are very happy that you did.'

'They are, they are. Of course at the time they thought I was interfering a little too much, but it all worked out well in the end.' She fell silent and shot him a glance.

'You looked happy on the dance floor with Miss Stanley.'

'I enjoy her company. More than I thought I would.'

'She needs to marry…you know that, don't you?'

'Of course.'

'I think she is still under the impression that she may get away with *not* getting married. She is hoping another scandal will happen and this will all just fade away.' Lady Mountjoy sighed and shook her head. 'Of course I hadn't expected there to be quite so much interest in your engagement. I think I underestimated how invested people are in your love life. I hear you are the most eligible bachelor in London, or at least you were before Miss Stanley ensnared you, as the gossips say.'

Sam shook his head, still unwilling to believe anyone thought him an eligible bachelor. He might have a title and a substantial income, but he barely spoke to the young women of society—surely they wanted someone they could get to know at least a little.

'I will talk to Miss Stanley, of course, make sure she understands that she will have to marry,' Lady Mountjoy said quietly, 'but I wanted to speak to you first.'

'Oh?'

'You and Miss Stanley are a handsome couple. Well matched in many ways.'

'We are complete opposites.'

'Yes, as are Lord Mountjoy and I, and we have enjoyed a long and happy marriage. Do you plan on marrying one day, Sam?'

'Yes.'

'And do you have a future wife in mind?'

'Good Lord, no.'

'Why not Miss Stanley, then?'

Sam closed his eyes. He'd known this was coming, known it from the very moment he had agreed to Lady Mountjoy's deception. The older woman wanted everyone paired off and as blissfully happy in marriage as she was.

'Miss Stanley and I want different things from life,' he said slowly, choosing his words carefully. He did not wish to be rude or offend, but he needed Lady Mountjoy to understand this wasn't a position he was going to change from. 'I want to live a quiet life in the country, to enjoy country pursuits, the occasional trip to town, the work I do with the orphanage and the other charities. I hope to travel one day, but of course I have the responsibilities of the estate and my tenants to look to first.'

He took a breath and had to banish an image of Eliza's smile from his mind as he pushed on. 'Miss Stanley wants nothing more than to be away from the countryside. She wants a life filled with adventure and excitement and everything she imagines the world has to offer her.'

'Is there more to it than that?'

'I saw what happened when two people with completely opposite and opposing priorities and personalities married. Neither of my parents was happy. My father spent his whole life trying to give my mother the excitement she wanted and ended up resenting her for it and my mother was never satisfied with what she had.' He shook his head. 'I will not be repeating their mistakes.'

'Miss Stanley says she wants adventure, but she is young. All she has experienced in life is a country existence in Somerset.'

'But doesn't she deserve the chance to work out for herself what she wants?'

'You know as well as I do that isn't how life works. I had hoped a quiet engagement to you and a discreet parting a few weeks later would be enough to save her, but now I am not so sure. If she remains unattached for too long after you two break your engagement, she may be seen as tainted. Her best hope is to marry.'

'Then perhaps she can find a husband who will give her all the adventure she desires.'

Lady Mountjoy reached over and patted him on the hand. 'Perhaps,' she said with a nod. 'I will encourage her to think about that. You think about your future, too, Sam. I want you to be happy.'

He nodded and watched as Lady Mountjoy left the room. For another minute he sat in the flickering candlelight, but then got up with a grunt of frustration. The idea of Eliza being forced to marry one of the bores of society was unpalatable, but it was better than the alternative.

Trying to forget about the whole thing completely, he left the small sitting room and returned to the ballroom.

He had barely re-entered the ballroom when he heard Eliza's sunny laugh and immediately his eyes were drawn towards her. She was dancing with a young gentleman he didn't know, but by the way his eyes roamed over her body it did not appear that he had honourable intentions.

For the next twenty minutes Sam prowled around the edge of the ballroom, not wanting to be drawn into the festivities, but knowing he could not yet make his escape. Only once was his gaze distracted by a group approaching him.

'I wanted to thank you again for your quick actions,' Mrs Appleby said as she made her way through the crowd, her two daughters flanking her on each side. 'I do not know how you spotted what was happening, but we are very grateful that you did.'

'It was my pleasure, Mrs Appleby.'

'I would like to offer my thanks, too,' Miss Amelia said, her voice a little high and nervous.

He didn't know the Applebys well, but had exchanged pleasantries with Mr Appleby once or twice before. The three women were all looking at him expectantly and he inclined his head at the younger Appleby daughter.

'No thanks are needed,' he said, wondering if he could pretend to hear someone calling him away.

'Are you enjoying the ball, Lord Thannock?' Miss Grace Appleby enquired, her face alight with excitement and glowing in the candlelight.

'It is diverting,' he said. 'How about you?'

'Oh, it is just wonderful. I do love to dance and the ballroom here at Haxby House is one of the grandest I have ever been in.'

Sam might try to avoid as many social occasions as he could, but he knew when a young woman was hoping to be asked to dance and Miss Appleby was looking at him with optimistic eyes.

'Would you care to dance, Miss Appleby?' He cursed himself even as the words came out, but he supposed it was better than standing on the edge of the dance floor as he counted the minutes until he could leave.

'Oh, I am honoured, Lord Thannock. I would enjoy that very much.'

It was a few minutes until the next dance, but when it was announced he dutifully found Miss Appleby and led her to a vacant spot. A few feet away Eliza was standing opposite a gentleman Sam didn't know, smiling at him as they waited for the music to start.

It was a quadrille and the music was lively. It was still relatively early in the evening so the room was abuzz with energy and excitement. Sam had danced many a quadrille and Miss Appleby was a competent partner so he didn't have to expend too much energy on concentrating on the dance.

Next to him was a couple he didn't recognise and he didn't pay them all that much attention. The woman had a cream-coloured dress on with the skirt made out of some floaty material. Every time she spun around the skirt puffed and spun through the air and once or twice he saw her partner have to catch himself to avoid stepping on it.

There wasn't that much chance for talking as it was such a lively dance, but Miss Appleby made a few comments as they came together, so he didn't see the whole sequence of events that unfolded next. All he heard was a strangled cry which he recognised immediately to be Eliza's.

He spun immediately to see her hurtling through the air. Tangled around her feet was a piece of cream-coloured fabric from the dress of the woman dancing next to him, which must have been stepped on and pulled off. Eliza flew spectacularly, her cry cut short as her face hit a metal urn holding an arrangement of flowers with a sickening thud.

'Eliza,' he shouted, dropping Miss Appleby's hand and darting towards Eliza as she lay unmoving on the round.

A space cleared around them as he crouched down and saw the trickle of blood from her forehead.

'I don't know what happened,' the woman with the cream dress was saying over and over again.

'Eliza,' he murmured, touching her gently on the shoulder. She was lying face down, half on her side, and he was reluctant to move her in case it did any more damage, but he knew she couldn't stay lying on the floor with everyone staring.

Carefully, he picked her up into his arms, noting with relief the rise and fall of her chest as he held her close and looked around for somewhere more comfortable to take her.

'I just don't know what happened.'

'She tripped on a stray piece of your dress,' Sam snapped, knowing it was unfair to blame the woman for her poorly designed outfit, but feeling angry with her all the same.

'Eliza,' he murmured again and felt the relief shoot through him when her eyes fluttered and a few seconds later a hand flew to her face.

'Ow,' she moaned, wriggling in his arms.

'Don't move, you've hit your head.'

After a few seconds she was able to focus on his eyes and he saw the flash of recognition there.

'Why are you carrying me?' she whispered.

'You were unconscious.'

Her hand delicately probed her forehead, her fingers coming away slick with blood, but she seemed more bothered by the area under her eye that was already starting to swell and turn an interesting purple colour.

'Where can I take her?' His question was directed to their hostess, Lady Haxby, who had arrived at his side and then nearly swooned at the sight of Eliza.

'Into my study,' Lord Haxby said quickly, motioning for Sam to follow him.

All eyes were on them as they left the ballroom.

'So much for letting ourselves fade from everyone's minds,' he muttered. The gossips would be talking about this for weeks.

The study was completely dark when they entered, but Lord Haxby quickly arranged for candles to be brought and sent a servant to see if there was any ice in the neighbouring houses to help bring down the bruising.

'What happened, my dear?' Lady Mountjoy called as she rushed into the room.

Sam was in the process of setting Eliza down on one of the armchairs, moving the pillows to ensure she was comfortable.

'I... I don't really know. My face hurts so much. I can't see. Is there something wrong with my eye?'

Sam saw Lady Mountjoy grimace and then pull herself together before she answered.

'Nothing that won't heal, my dear, I'm sure.'

'She tripped. Some woman's dress was floating about all over the place and a piece of the fabric got caught around Eliza's legs.'

'Oh, how awful for you.'

'I will send for the doctor,' Lord Haxby said.

'Thank you.' Lady Mountjoy came and sat next to Eliza, brushing her hair from her face in a motherly way.

Sam stepped back, suddenly feeling awkward. He had acted instinctively, swooping in and picking Eliza up, carrying her through the crowded ballroom to somewhere more private, but now everyone else was rallying around he felt superfluous.

'Sam... Lord Thannock,' Eliza called, reaching out her hand to him. Coming to crouch down beside her, he took her soft hand in his. 'Thank you for carrying me here.'

'Any time, Miss Stanley.'

For a long moment she kept hold of his hand, only relinquishing it when Lady Mountjoy coughed and gave her a hard look.

Chapter Nine

'I'm quite happy to stay with you and keep you company,' Jane said, looking wistfully at the book Eliza had in her hands.

'As am I,' Lucy said quickly. 'There are so many balls and dances I truly do not mind missing one or two.'

'I will not hear of it,' Eliza said quickly. 'I am well set up here with one of Jane's books. You must go and dance and have a wonderful time so you can come back and tell me all about it.'

'You could come,' Jane said kindly. 'The swelling around your eye is much better today and the bruising hardly noticeable.'

In the corner of the room, Miss Huntley snorted. 'Hardly noticeable in a darkened room perhaps,' she muttered.

'Why do you have to be so mean all the time?' Lucy snapped, making Eliza and Jane sit up straighter. Lucy was normally the sweetest-natured person among them and the most tolerant of Miss Huntley's snide comments.

'I am not mean, I am truthful,' Miss Huntley said primly.

'You are cruel and it is unnecessary. We have to spend so much time together—surely it would be easier for everyone if you at least tried to be pleasant.'

'You are all just far too sensitive,' Miss Huntley said, standing and stalking from the room.

Silence followed for a few seconds as they waited to check Miss Huntley wasn't going to burst back into the room.

'Is something amiss, Lucy?' Eliza enquired gently.

'Something needed to be said to her—she has been nothing but mean ever since we all met in Somerset.'

'I do not disagree,' Eliza said, choosing her words carefully. She knew she often rushed in and said something unwise that wasn't entirely thought through and she didn't want to say anything to upset Lucy. 'But normally it would be me snapping at Miss Huntley and you the voice of reason.'

Lucy gave a sudden little sob and threw herself into Eliza's arms.

'What on earth is the matter?' Eliza said softly, wrapping her friend in her arms and rubbing her back in the way her mother used to do to her when she was upset.

Lucy sniffled. 'I haven't heard from William for ten weeks and I'm worried something has happened.'

Eliza bit her lip. Before their journey to London, Lucy had confided in her and Jane that she was already secretly engaged to a young man she had known all her life. He was the youngest son of Sir Thomas Weyman and the engagement was having to be kept secret because Sir Thomas had made it clear he would expect a better match for his son than the local vicar's daughter. William Weyman had followed in his father's footsteps and was currently serving as an officer in the army, sending sporadic letters home to Lucy, promising to marry her when he next returned home.

'Oh, Lucy,' Eliza said, not wanting to dismiss her friend's concern, but knowing she didn't need to hear a list of all the things that could have gone wrong. Right now it was her job to give reassurance. 'You know what post is like from Europe, it could take months to reach us, and then it would probably be sent to your home address. I know you sent on our new address in London, but there is no guarantee William even received it.'

'I know, I know. It is foolish to be this worried, but I have this bad feeling deep inside that something has happened to him.'

'Your mother is writing to you, isn't she?'

'Yes, but she doesn't know of our attachment.'

'William is a friend from childhood, is he not? If there was some big news about him, do you not think your mother would let you know?'

'I suppose.'

'Then I think we can blame the postal system.'

Lucy nodded and then groaned. 'Do I need to apologise to Miss Huntley?'

'Good Lord, no. You said nothing that wasn't deserved.'

Eliza squeezed Lucy in for a tighter hug and then let her go, watching as she and Jane put the finishing touches to their appearances for the evening.

'Are you all ready?' Lady Mountjoy said as she swept into the room looking as perfectly coiffed as ever. 'Oh, Eliza darling, your poor eye. Are you happy staying here tonight?'

'I will not pretend I'm not a little jealous,' Eliza said, managing a smile, 'but have fun and hopefully I will be able to join you again soon.'

'Get some rest.'

'I will. Have a good evening.'

The house seemed quiet once the Mountjoys, Jane, Lucy and Miss Huntley had all left and Eliza was aware it would be easy to sink into a bout of melancholy. For a while she prowled around, wandering into the library and selecting a few different books from the shelves to add to the one Jane had given her and then trailing from room to room to decide on the best place to sit. She enjoyed reading to a degree, but knew she lacked the ability to sit still and concentrate for long periods of time like Jane had to make her an avid reader.

Still, she was quite enjoying giggling at the rules in *A Gentlewoman's Guide to Etiquette* when she heard a knock on the front door.

It was far too late for visitors, at least any of the salubrious sort, so curiosity was pricked. She listened carefully as a footman hurried from downstairs, pulling on his jacket as he went past the drawing room, and opened the door.

There was a low voice, too low for Eliza to make out the words and then the inaudible reply of the footman as he mumbled something. *Useless*, Eliza thought, rising from her chair and thinking she would take a peek at the caller.

As she moved to the door she almost collided with the broad figure coming through it and felt his hands immediately on her arms to catch her if she stumbled.

'Steady,' Sam's deep voice cautioned, and Eliza felt a little skip in her pulse as he smiled down at her. From this close she could smell his scent—there was just a hint of something earthy mixed with a fresher, citrusy tone. She had the urge to bury her face in his neck and inhale deeply, but caught herself before she could do anything so ridiculous.

'What are you doing here?'

'I've come to see the invalid.'

'Hardly an invalid...' she motioned to herself '...more a mess.'

'Let me have a look at you.' Sam took her by the hand and led her over to stand by a set of three candles on the mantelpiece. Eliza heard the little gasp that escaped from her lips as his fingers gently touched her chin and tilted her head to one side. For a long moment he studied her eye and the bruise that had formed around it.

'*That* is a beauty.'

'It's horrific. Lady Mountjoy said I had better stay in until it fades enough to be concealed with some powder.'

'That may take a few weeks, although I would say the bruising has all come out now and the swelling looks as though it has started to go down.'

'How do you know about bruised eyes?'

Sam shrugged. 'I've done a little boxing in the past. Taken a few hits.'

'Boxing?' Eliza laughed and then saw he was serious. 'I can't imagine you boxing.'

'It is good exercise and sometimes it just feels good to hit something.'

He was still holding her chin, his fingers resting lightly on her skin, and Eliza didn't want to move, she didn't want anything to break this moment. She knew it was ridiculous, he was inspecting her bruised eye, not reading her poetry and whispering sweet nothings in her ear, but still she felt an irresistible pull.

She didn't want to examine it, didn't want to think about it any deeper than the primal, visceral level she was being pulled to him on. Right now she wanted to forget this was Sam, the last man she should be feeling any attraction for, and lose herself to the exquisite anticipation.

For a long moment his eyes held hers, flicking focus from one to the other as if searching for something in them. Then, with a sharp intake of breath, he stepped away.

Eliza felt bereft and had to tilt her head down so he wouldn't see the disappointment in her eyes.

'You shouldn't be here, Sam,' Eliza said, turning away.

'I know, but I was worried about you.'

'Careful, or you'll start behaving like a real fiancé.'

'When you fell...' he said, then shook his head and forced a smile to his lips. 'Tonight I knew you would be moping.'

'I was not moping. Before you came and interrupted I was having a very pleasant evening reading about etiquette.'

'Etiquette?' He raised an eyebrow and a smile quirked his lips. Eliza was struck by how attractive he was when he smiled and it took a few moments for the question to register in her brain.

'I am fast learning that etiquette is *the backbone of society* and without it *civilisation would crumble*.'

'Fascinating as your book sounds, I thought I would offer my services in keeping you entertained.'

Suddenly, Eliza's mouth felt completely dry and she struggled to swallow. She felt the heat blossom in her cheeks and silently gave thanks for the muted candle-light that would hide her blushes. Of course he didn't mean *that*.

An image of Sam's lips brushing against hers filled her mind and it was impossible for her to think of anything else. As he took a step towards her, she felt her own lips part and she almost smacked herself in the face when she quickly raised a hand to cover them.

'I thought I would teach you to play the piano.'

'In one evening?'

He smiled. 'Well, we could at least make a start. Would you like that?'

'Yes. Very much.'

Lady Mountjoy had a beautiful grand piano sitting in the corner of the drawing room and she had told all of the debutantes they were welcome to play when-ever the fancy took them. Miss Huntley would often sit down and play a piece perfectly, looking pleased with her efforts. In the main Eliza had tried to stay as far away from the piano in case anyone asked her to play, but once or twice she had trailed her fingers over the ivory keys and wondered what it would be like to know how to put the notes together to play more than one piece of music.

In the few seconds it took her to walk over to the piano Eliza gave herself a stern talking to. This was Sam, kind and generous Sam, but not someone she should be fantasising about kissing. He might be her pretend fiancé for a few more weeks, but he had made it very clear after that they would be going their separate ways. Besides, he wasn't what she wanted from her future. Kissing him might be what she wanted right now, but settling down with him into the routine of country life most certainly wasn't.

As she took a deep, shaky breath, all her resolve almost fled as he sat down next to her on the piano stool. They were so close Eliza could feel the heat of Sam's body even through all the layers of clothes.

'First of all have a feel of the keys,' he said, placing a hand on the piano and pressing down on one key after another in turn.

Eliza copied, a little further down the piano.

'Good. Now, the most important note to learn is this one.' He picked up her hand in his own and moved it so her thumb rested where he wanted it to be. Eliza felt a spark of energy jump between them and found it hard to concentrate on his words. 'This is middle C. If you can remember this note, then you can work out any other note on the piano.'

He showed her how to play the notes with each finger in turn, demonstrating first and then helping her with positioning before letting her have a go on her own.

'Shall we learn a simple tune?'

'Already?'

'Yes. It's the first thing children are normally taught on the piano when they take lessons.' He swayed even closer and Eliza felt his arm brush against her breast as he helped her position her hands. 'Copy me,' he said, 'On the same notes, just further down.'

It took five minutes for her to learn the little tune, and although it was what was taught to children, she felt a swell of accomplishment.

'I've got something to continue your studies until our next lesson,' Sam said with a smile. He brought a sheet of music out of his jacket pocket and unfolded it.

'Oh? I feel like a child in the schoolroom.'

'You're hardly that,' he murmured so quietly Eliza thought she wasn't meant to hear. 'Here. I've marked the notes on the first line. You go through and work out all the other notes from what I've done already.'

'You're actually setting me work to do?'

'Yes. It'll be good for you, stop you fretting about that eye.'

'It's not as though I'm sitting around moping, staring in the mirror all day long.'

'Good, then you'll have plenty of time to do this.' He handed her the sheet. She looked down at it and shook her head in disbelief.

'Do you think anyone else's fake fiancé sets them work to do?'

'No. I think you're just lucky I care so much. Just think, at the end of this you'll be saved from scandal *and* you'll be able to play the piano.'

'You are unbelievable. Does anyone else know you're like this?'

Sam grinned at her again. 'No. I try to keep a stony facade when I am out in public.'

'Why?'

He shuddered. 'Far too many interested debutantes.'

'I thought that was what you wanted. To settle down with a perfect wife in the country and raise a perfect little family away from the hustle and bustle of London.'

'You've been speaking to Lady Mountjoy.'

'She has been dropping a lot of information about you into our conversations.'

'Oh?'

'I know things that you've never told me.'

'Like what?'

'You graduated with a double first from Oxford in Classics and Latin.'

'Sunt optimus annorum vitae meae.'

'Stop showing off. I know that you support no less than five charitable establishments, including two orphanages. You also ensure you are in Parliament for all the important votes even though you would much rather be at your country estate. You are beloved by your tenants and your servants and probably even the man who comes to set your clocks.'

Sam held up his hands. 'Enough.' He laughed. 'Lady Mountjoy really is trying to promote my good qualities, isn't she?'

'Is it all true?'

He shrugged. 'I don't know that the man who comes to set my clocks *loves* me...'

Eliza swatted him on the arm. 'You are a saint—I knew it.'

'Not a saint.' He held her eye for a moment and Eliza felt a thrill of anticipation pulse through her. In the flickering candlelight it was difficult to see the finer detail of his expression, but Eliza felt the atmosphere in the room change as his arm brushed against hers. Ever so slowly, as if he was trying to talk himself out of it, he brought his fingers to her face, shifting his position so now his body was angled towards hers.

Eliza felt as though she couldn't breathe properly. Every rational thought deserted her and all she could focus on was what Sam might do next.

Softly, he groaned and then leaned forward, catching the back of her head with his hand and drawing her in towards him. As his lips brushed against hers Eliza instinctively pressed forward even further, deepening the kiss.

It was her first kiss and it was everything she had ever imagined it might be.

Sam's fingers tangled in her hair, and Eliza felt little sparks of excitement shoot through her body. His other hand was trailing over her back, and she gasped as he reached the neckline of her dress and touched skin. In that one moment she wanted to abandon herself to him, to invite him to do all the things her body was yearning for, all the things she knew were forbidden.

His lips lingered on hers, as if he were savouring the

moment, his fingertips moving to caress her cheek as she pressed her body against his.

Eliza didn't know if it was the movement that shocked Sam back to reality, or something else, but suddenly he stiffened and then recoiled as if he had been shot.

For a long moment he could do nothing more than look at her, confusion and bewilderment in his eyes. Eliza tried not to show how much his reaction to their kiss hurt her, but she knew the betrayal was evident in her expression. Finally, she turned away, standing and moving to the other side of the room and fiddling with the curtains to give her hands something to do so Sam wouldn't see them shaking.

'Eliza,' he said eventually, none of the levity from a few minutes earlier in his voice.

She shook her head, refusing to turn around. She wasn't sure what she felt right at that moment, but she knew how she had felt when he kissed her and she didn't want to hear him dismiss that.

'Eliza, look at me.'

'No.'

He must have crossed the room silently for the next thing Eliza knew his hand was gently but firmly in the small of her back, showing her he wasn't going anywhere until she had acknowledged whatever it was he wanted her to acknowledge.

'I'm sorry,' Sam said quietly. 'I shouldn't have done that, I shouldn't have come here, not when I knew you would be alone.'

'Don't apologise,' she said sharply, then looked up into his eyes. It was a mistake and Eliza felt a stab of pain shoot through her body, enough to almost take her breath away. She couldn't force out any more words so she wriggled free of his touch and moved as fast as she could towards the door. Without a backwards glance she slipped out of the drawing room and ran up the stairs, gathering her skirts about her so she could move faster. Sam wouldn't dare to follow her upstairs, but even so she didn't slow down until she was in her bedroom with the door firmly closed behind her.

Chapter Ten

Sam leaned low over Copper's back and urged his horse to gallop even faster. The morning air was cold and crisp with just the hint of fog near the water. It was bracing, and Sam felt it waken all of his senses and help him shake off the last remnants of sleep. Not that he had slept the last two nights. Every time he'd closed his eyes he'd been back in the drawing room with Eliza, sitting with her at the piano, allowing himself to lean in and kiss her even though he knew it was the worst possible thing he could do.

'Wait up, Thannock,' his friend called from a distance.

Sam slowed a little, allowing the other man to catch up and his horse to fall into step besides Copper. Viscount Townsend was Lord and Lady Mountjoy's son and Sam's good friend for many years.

'You're running from something, Thannock.'

Sam smiled at him, but was aware the smile didn't quite meet his eyes.

'You've got slow now you're a happily married man, Townsend.'

Tom laughed good naturedly. Sam didn't think he had once seen his friend truly upset about anything.

They rode on in silence for a few minutes, appreciating the morning view and the quiet in the normally busy park.

'My mother has embroiled you in one of her plans, hasn't she?' Tom said as they lifted their hats in greeting to a group of three young men out for a morning ride.

'Why do you say that?' He thought of Eliza and realised embroiled was exactly the right word to use for his involvement in her life.

'She was gushing about you this morning at breakfast and kept sneaking looks at one of the young ladies. Miss Summers or Miss Stanmore, something beginning with S.'

'Miss Stanley.' Even though he was on horseback, Sam closed his eyes for a moment and tried to banish the feeling of panic that swept over him when he thought of Eliza. It was all such a mess.

'Is she matchmaking or something worse?'

'Something worse.'

Tom raised an eyebrow in enquiry and Sam sighed. It would do no harm to confide in his friend. Tom was only planning on staying in London for a few days, a quick visit to conduct some business before returning to his wife and his country estate in a couple of days. It was to be so brief he hadn't even bothered opening up his own town house, opting to spend a few nights at Lord and Lady Mountjoy's house instead.

'Miss Stanley found herself in a spot of bother. A darkened room, an ill-advised acquaintance with Lord Wilson…' He trailed off. He could still see the panic in her eyes when he had burst in on them that first night.

'He's always been an animal.'

'He left without too much bother, but I stayed to ensure she was not too shaken and then we were discovered, just the two of us.'

'In a compromising position?'

'No, nothing like that, but you know how the *ton* likes to make something out of nothing.'

'You agreed to marry her?' Tom sounded surprised.

'No. At least not in reality. I agreed to the pretence of an engagement for a few weeks.'

Tom looked at him long and hard, his eyes assessing him in much the way Lady Mountjoy's did. The familial resemblance was uncanny.

'Either Miss Stanley is a complete nightmare to spend any amount of time with or you've fallen for her.'

Sam let out a splutter. 'I haven't fallen for her.'

'And she didn't seem a nightmare. Engaging, sharp and observant and pretty to boot.'

'I haven't fallen for her.'

'What has you trying to outrace your thoughts, then?'

Sam sighed. There weren't many people he shared any of his deeper thoughts with. It was a way of protecting himself, he knew that, but hadn't ever tried to change over the years. When he was younger there hadn't been anyone to confide his feelings or secrets in, so as he got older he hadn't sought out anyone to change that. Tom, however, had a way of burrowing in, with his easy charm and friendly affability.

'We may have shared a kiss.'

'Ah. And this kiss was terrible?'

'No.'

'I see.'

'It was ill advised, reckless, irresponsible. It will not be repeated.'

Tom remained silent for a long moment, clearly choosing his words carefully before speaking again. 'Does Miss Stanley know this?'

Sam inhaled deeply. He had never planned on kissing her, but if he was completely honest the urge to take her in his arms had been building since their first meeting. For the past couple of weeks he had been in denial about his attraction, but the attraction had been present and ever-growing and he now knew Miss Stanley had felt the same. A woman couldn't kiss a man like that and not feel *anything*.

After the kiss he'd left too abruptly. He should have stayed, asked a maid to cajole Miss Stanley back downstairs, thrashed out the remorse and self-recrimination there and then, before hopefully settling into a truce where they both agreed to focus on riding out the scandal that tied them together and quietly finding a way to move on with their lives.

'I can see your dilemma,' Tom said, gazing out across the gently rolling green hills towards the water. 'You have a pretty and engaging young woman who you are attracted to, who also is attracted to you. You are engaged in the eyes of the *ton*. One day you wish to have a wife to help you carry on the Thannock family name.' He quirked an eyebrow at Sam. 'Wait, did I say I saw your dilemma?'

'We are not well suited,' Sam said, trying to forget how perfectly she fit into his arms. Two nights ago they had felt well suited.

'Why ever not?'

'You're starting to sound like your mother.'

'Wise woman my mother, especially when it comes to affairs of the heart.'

Sam closed his eyes for a few seconds and took a moment to consider what his friend was suggesting. He knew he could argue that Eliza wanted more than he could offer her, that he could foresee the past repeating itself, with him and Eliza trapped in a discontented union like his parents. He didn't want that for either of them, and it was enough of a reason in itself, but he knew if he was being entirely honest there was more to it than that.

If he were to get married, he would not risk his heart on someone who was not completely committed to the idea of being his wife. He had felt the pain of being second or third best from his mother, but also his father who had always chosen Lady Thannock or his work over his son. Sam would not voluntarily ever put himself in that position again. *If* he married, he would make sure the woman wanted nothing more than to be his wife and companion, and later the devoted mother to his children.

'I need to speak to her,' Sam said quietly. 'I need to make sure she understands.'

'Try not to worry, old chap. These things have a way of working themselves out. Look on the bright side—at least you're not the girl. You break off the engagement and everyone will think nothing less of you, but if she does she will be shunned.'

'What a mess,' Sam said more to himself than Tom.

'Life can be messy. Fancy a race to the Serpentine? Loser can buy drinks at the club later.'

Glad of the distraction, Sam urged on his horse, leaning low over the animal's neck, trying to concentrate on the rhythm of its hooves and the feel of the wind in his hair rather than Eliza's face before she had fled from the drawing room the night before.

Chapter Eleven

Eliza didn't know what she imagined London to look like in the snow, perhaps grimy and grey from the dirt of the city, but as she gazed longingly out of the window at the empty street below she had to acknowledge it was beautiful.

It helped that it was not yet eight in the morning and the snow had fallen thick and fast overnight. There were a few tracks where people had walked down the pavement, and one set of hoof prints, but otherwise the snow lay undisturbed.

If she were at home, Eliza would already be lacing up her skates and heading out to the little pond at the edge of the village, eager to be the first one to make tracks across the ice. Here, in London, she wasn't even sure if skating was an acceptable pastime and if it was she wouldn't know where to go about finding the best spot. For the first time since arriving in London Eliza felt a pang of homesickness, but quickly smothered it. She knew much of the problem was she was stuck inside still, the bruises beneath her eyes fading to a pale purple, but not easy to cover all the same.

Tracing the outline of a star in the condensation on the window, Eliza sighed quietly. Her seclusion wasn't the only thing that was bothering her, but she refused to spend any more time fretting over Sam.

'You're up early,' Jane said, her voice heavy with sleep as she shifted in the bed they shared in a comfortable bedroom in Lord and Lady Mountjoy's town house.

'I caught a glimpse of the snow through a crack in the curtains,' Eliza said, turning her head away from the window for a moment. 'I couldn't resist coming to have a peek.'

'Is it thick?' Jane made no move to get out of bed, and Eliza could tell she was already dropping back off to sleep. Normally, she and Jane were well suited to share a room, both preferring to sleep in as late as possible, even eschewing breakfast on occasion in favour of half an hour extra in bed.

'It looks beautiful.'

There was no reply from Jane except heavy breathing.

Eliza stood silently and picked up her shawl from where she had placed it the evening before on the back of a chair. Wrapping it around her shoulders, she slipped out of the room and headed downstairs, wondering if Lucy might be up and about but loathe to knock on the door to the bedroom she shared with Miss Huntley.

The maids were bustling about downstairs, sweeping out the grates and laying the fires ready for the day ahead. Eliza watched with mild interest, finding the scratch of the bristles of the brushes on the grate strangely soothing. At home it would often fall to Eliza to set the fire. In more recent years they had been able to afford a maid, but it hadn't always been the case and Eliza had grown up learning to chop vegetables, scrub floors as well as a hundred other household jobs.

Pulling her shawl around her shoulders, Eliza found a comfortable spot in the corner of the library, curled up in an armchair and allowed her eyes to grow heavy while she watched the maid work.

Eliza felt disorientated when she awoke three hours later. The house was strangely quiet and for a moment she didn't know where she was. Her neck and shoulders were stiff from dropping off to sleep in an awkward position and she had to shake her hand for half a minute before any feeling returned to her fingers.

She stood, stretching out her protesting muscles, and listened for a minute. The door to the library was closed, but even so the house didn't sound like it normally would in the mornings.

Walking out into the hallway, Eliza found herself wishing she had put on slippers before her early-morning trip downstairs. The floor was icy and she was forced to walk on tiptoes until she reached one of the plush rugs. Glancing in at the dining room, she could see breakfast had already been cleared away and she wondered quite how long she had slept for in the armchair in the library.

Finally, she spied a footman carrying a heavy vase up the servant's stairs and called out, 'Where is everyone?'

'They have all gone out skating, miss,' he said, resting the vase on the banister as he paused to speak to her.

'Oh.' Eliza felt a pang of disappointment. 'How long ago did they leave?'

'Half an hour, miss. Her ladyship wanted to go before the ice became slushy and melted. Miss Ashworth and Miss Freeman did talk about waking you, but Lady Mountjoy said to let you rest.' The footman gave her a lopsided smile. 'Would you like me to ask Cook to do you some breakfast, miss?'

Eliza hesitated, but knew there was no point in sulking. Everyone had gone out to enjoy the ice and snow and once again she was left behind. First she'd been forced to stay in until Sam could be persuaded to come to her rescue with the fake engagement and now she was trapped in the house until the bruising on her face subsided. It would be easy to feel sorry for herself.

'That would be lovely, yes, please.'

She was about to go upstairs and dress before breakfast when there was a light rap on the front door. Conscious she was clad only in her nightclothes, although they covered her from neck to ankle and couldn't be called anything but modest, Eliza darted back into the library, listening as the footman opened the door. She felt a sense of events repeating themselves as she remembered the late-night visit from Sam a couple of days ago that had started in exactly this manner.

'Please make yourself comfortable, my lord, I will enquire whether Miss Stanley is accepting visitors.'

Eliza heard footsteps down the hall and as she peeked

around the door frame saw Sam's familiar figure stepping through the door into the drawing room.

She felt her heart skip a beat and she had to quickly dart back into the shadows of the library as she heard herself make an involuntary gasp. She hated that her initial, visceral reaction was one of joy and anticipation—it made it so much harder to stay aloof and distant.

Certain she did not want to see Sam today, she waited for a moment and then crept quietly out of the library and along the hall. She had to pass the drawing room to reach the stairs and all she could do was hope that he was facing away from the door.

Taking a deep breath, she hurried past and reached the stairs, using the banister to swing herself round on to the bottom step. As she was readying herself to dash up the stairs, she felt a hand on her wrist and stiffened, foot halfway in the air.

'Eliza,' Sam murmured, his expression one of surprise. 'I'm sorry, I did not know you were yet to dress for the day.'

His eyes raked over her body, and she felt a terrible heat beginning at her centre and spreading like fire in a forest.

'I needed to see you.' He was yet to relinquish her wrist and Eliza was secretly glad. She knew if he let go she would have to flee upstairs and she wasn't quite ready for that yet.

Forcing herself to remember the look in his eyes once he had come to his senses after their kiss, she gave him a haughty look.

'I don't see what there is to say to one another.'

'Eliza.'

With a sag of her shoulders she relented. 'Will you at least let me get dressed first?'

His eyes darted down to her nightgown. 'I think that might be a good idea.'

'Where is everyone else?' Sam asked as Eliza re-appeared thirty minutes later. He wasn't sure if it normally took her that long to get ready in the morning, or if she had been going extra slow to make him wait, but gone was the beautifully dishevelled look from half an hour earlier and in its place a perfectly coiffed version of Eliza.

He tried to suppress the thought that he liked her just as much, or even more perhaps, in her natural state and told himself firmly that he had no right to see or think about her like that.

'Ice skating.'

'You didn't wish to go?'

She motioned at the bruising now fading underneath her eyes.

'I don't pretend to know anything about the creams and powders available for women, but surely there is something that could cover the bruising.'

'We tried last night with some powder, but it was too tender to cover properly.'

Sam knew she would not have given up easily. It must be difficult for such a vibrant and sociable young woman to be cooped up like this while everyone else was out enjoying themselves.

'I've hated missing out on everything, but this is the absolute worst.'

'Oh?'

'I *love* to skate, that freedom you feel whizzing over the ice, it is like no other feeling in the world.'

Sam watched as she closed her eyes for a moment, no doubt imagining herself wherever it was she had gained her love of skating.

'I'm sorry I have not come before now,' he said quietly once she had refocused on him.

'There is no need…'

He reached out and placed a hand over the top of hers. 'There is, Eliza. I behaved poorly in many ways and I think we need to talk about it. We still have a lot of time to spend together and I do not want this ruse of ours to fail because I could not keep control of my desires.'

Eliza's eyes flicked up and met his as he mentioned his desire and he wondered if being completely honest with her was the right course.

'The other night, when we were sitting at the piano, I couldn't help but kiss you,' he said softly, aware even now his eyes were flicking from hers to her lips and an unconscious part of him was thinking about kissing her again. 'We were sitting close and I was enjoying myself more than I have in a long time. I *needed* to kiss you.' He shook his head, knowing he wasn't explaining himself well.

'I felt it, too,' Eliza said ever so quietly.

He nodded, and a wave of understanding passed between them. They had both felt it, that irrepressible urge to kiss, to join together and never let go.

'As a gentleman, I should have stopped myself, but I didn't, and for that I apologise.'

She quirked a little smile at him. 'I think you are the only man I know who would make sure I knew you were apologising for not suppressing your desire rather than having the desire in the first place.'

'I do not think we can blame ourselves for an emotion that comes naturally.'

'No.'

'More than that, I should apologise for how I acted after.' He raked a hand through his hair and then smiled at her. 'I don't know how a man is meant to act when he's kissed an innocent young woman he's pretending to be engaged to, but I am sure I could have done better.'

'I suppose it is a strange situation for us both.'

'It is.'

They sat in silence for a long moment, but it felt less awkward than before.

Eliza gave him a mischievous smile and Sam felt something settle inside him. 'Are you thinking about kissing me now?'

'Miss Eliza Stanley, you should come with a warning.'

'You didn't answer my question.'

He cleared his throat, now unable to think of anything but kissing her.

'You are, aren't you?' She sounded half-shocked, half-gleeful.

'I might be,' he conceded, 'but nothing can happen, you know that, don't you, Eliza?'

The smile dropped from her face, the atmosphere in the room serious once more. 'I know.'

'I can't marry you, no matter how much I like you.'

'Please don't get the wrong impression,' Eliza said slowly, looking down at her hands. 'I'm not fishing for a real proposal or anything like that, but surely you are free to marry whomever you want.'

Sam nodded, knowing they had to have this talk, but not sure he wanted to ruin the closeness there was between them.

'You're right. I am free to marry whomever I want.'

'So it is the idea of being married to me that sends you running?'

'No, you are a wonderful woman, Eliza, and I think one day you will make some man very happy as his wife, but I think our priorities in life, our wants and needs and dreams, are so different that we would make each other unhappy.' He paused and smiled at her. 'I want you to be happy, Eliza.'

'Lady Mountjoy has told me I will need to marry if I want to continue with this life in London.'

'You have options.'

'None of them that appealing. I marry someone I barely know or I return to Somerset to the life I was so desperate to leave behind.'

He nodded, and she gave him a smile that didn't quite reach her eyes.

'Do not fear—as I said, I am not pressing you for marriage.'

'I like you, Eliza, more than I should, but I think you can see we are poorly matched.'

'You say that a lot.'

'I grew up living with a couple who were so poorly

matched it made them both miserable. I do not want that.'

He searched her face for some clue as to what she was thinking, but for once her emotions were not visible.

'I think before two people enter a union that will tie them together for life there should be an acknowledgement of what they want from their lives. Of course no two people's aims and hopes are ever completely the same, but general values should match.'

'And ours don't,' Eliza said, a note of sadness in her voice.

'Ours don't.'

For a long moment they just sat there, both not quite ready to move on. Suddenly, Eliza grinned and moved a little closer. 'Then we will have to strive never to be in a position where you might want to kiss me again.'

He looked down at her lips and had to suppress a groan. Never before had he met anyone who affected him on a primal, subconscious level like Eliza did.

'Minx.'

She leaned in even closer so their lips were only inches apart and then sat back with a laugh.

'Come on,' Sam said, standing up.

'You forget I am in seclusion until my face is less likely to offend the delicate sensibilities of the *ton*.'

'Nonsense. They can look away if they feel offended by you.'

'We're really going out?'

'Unless you don't want to skate on the canal in St James's Park?'

'Give me five minutes,' she said, jumping up from her seat with renewed vigour, almost out of the room before she paused. 'I don't have any skates in London.'

'I've come prepared. I have a pair for us both.'

Chapter Twelve

Eliza smiled up at Sam as they walked arm in arm towards St James's Park. He was a hard man to remain angry with, and even though she still felt a little wounded when she thought of how he had initially reacted to their kiss, she couldn't deny his reasons for doing so were sound.

She glanced at him again, wondering whether it was normal to feel a warm glow inside when she remembered how he had admitted how much he wanted to kiss her. Their acquaintance was destined to be nothing more than a friendship, yet it gave her a thrill to know he felt that same flare of attraction and desire as she did whenever he was near.

'Am I going to have to hold you up on the ice?'

She raised a haughty eyebrow and gave him a superior look. 'I think it more likely I shall be supporting you.'

'You are that confident?'

'I suggest a wager,' Eliza said, feeling her excitement

rise as they entered the park, the canal visible in the distance.

'A wager? What are the terms?'

'I think we should wager on who takes a tumble first.'

'Agreed. And the prize?'

'If I win, you agree to attend the Willinghams' masquerade ball with me tomorrow evening, no more protestations.'

Sam groaned, and Eliza couldn't help but laugh. She had been trying to persuade him to accompany her to the masquerade ball since they had started to negotiate which engagements they would attend together, but Sam had always been reluctant.

'And if I win?'

'What would you like as your prize?'

Eliza felt the heat flood to her cheeks as his eyes raked over her for a moment and then he whispered in her ear, 'If I win, not only do we *not* attend the Willinghams' masquerade ball, but we forgo any further masquerades of the Season.'

'What is it you have against masquerades?'

'They are ridiculous. What is the point of them? No one wears a disguise decent enough to afford them anonymity, but there is meant to be an air of mystery about the event. It doesn't make any sense.'

'Calm down, no one is forcing you to attend. *Yet.*'

'You will not be laughing so much when you are looking up at me from your *derrière* on the ice, pleading with me to help you up.'

Eliza swallowed hard, suddenly overwhelmed by an

image of Sam leaning over her not on the ice, but in the bedroom. Quickly, she pushed it out of her mind, hoping Sam hadn't noticed the lapse in her concentration.

'Don't think I will be pulling you up when you are in a tangle of limbs,' she said.

The park was busy even though it was still before noon. The lure of the snow and frozen-over waterways was too much for many of the London residents, especially as this was the first proper snow of the season.

As they approached the canal, they saw lots of people out on the ice, some much more confident than others. It was mainly groups of young men, but there were a few couples venturing out now, too, and no one seemed overly interested in Sam and Eliza as they began pulling on the skates Sam had brought with him.

'May I be of assistance?'

'Is it allowed?' Eliza was looking surreptitiously at the other people gathered along the edge of the canal to see if any other young lady was allowing her partner to fasten her skates.

'It is more than allowed, it is expected a gentleman will help a lady with her skates.'

Eliza watched as Sam crouched, gently helping her raise her boot and slip it into the base of the skate before lacing it on tight. His fingers brushed against her ankle, and she felt a jolt of energy ripple over her skin from the contact.

'There, can you balance?'

They were only a few steps from the ice, but Eliza knew this was always the trickiest part of ice skating, that transition from solid ground, down the bank and on to the ice.

She nodded, watching as Sam expertly strapped on his own skates. He laced them as if he did so every day and Eliza wondered whether their wager might not be so easily won as she had first imagined.

'I'll step down first,' he said, testing the ice out with his skate, 'and then I will help you down.'

It was a little drop from the bank, and Eliza was glad of his steadying hand as she touched her skate down on to the ice. It wasn't awfully busy, but there was already some slush where the skaters had been before them, and Eliza had to take a moment to find her balance.

'Would you like me to hold you?' Sam said with a quirk of his brow.

Eliza ignored him, straightened and pushed off with her skates, knowing the worst thing you could do on the ice was hesitate.

For a moment, as she pushed away from the bank and closed her eyes, Eliza felt as though she were flying. It was pure bliss and she never wanted the feeling to stop, but she knew she had to open her eyes, to come back to reality or risk falling.

Without looking back to check Sam was following her, she whizzed down the canal, glad for once that everybody was too engrossed in their own fun to be taking much notice of her.

'You skate well, Eliza,' Sam said, his breath tickling her ear. She hadn't realised he had stayed so close and felt a shiver run down her spine as he placed a hand in the small of her back.

She looked down and watched his easy movements on the ice, as natural to him as dancing, and reached out to take his arm.

'So do you,' she said, slowing for a moment. 'Will you skate with me?'

They skated a little farther up the canal, stopping when the ice looked to be a little thinner and turning back. Neither of them had the desire to plunge into the cold water below.

'There's no one watching us,' Sam said, and Eliza looked around to see he was right. There was no one on the banks here and no other skaters close by. 'Will you dance with me?'

'Dance?'

'A waltz?'

'There's no music,' Eliza said with a laugh.

'We don't need it.'

Sam slipped one arm around her waist and Eliza adjusted her grip on his hand and then did something she had never done before: she let someone else take control of her movements on the ice. Back home she had always skated alone, relishing the freedom, the sensation of gliding faster than she could ever run. It had always been a solo pursuit.

At first they moved smoothly but slowly, getting used to trusting one another on the ice, but after a minute or two Eliza felt Sam adjust his grip a little and they really began to skate properly. As he twirled her and then caught her Eliza felt a happiness she hadn't before and wondered if they could keep dancing on the ice for ever.

'We should stop,' Sam said as he pulled her in closer towards him. 'We're getting an audience.'

Glancing up, Eliza saw the huddle of ladies and gentlemen on the bank, watching them with surprised expressions. There were one or two faces she knew, but still so many people in their social circle in London were strangers to her.

'One more minute,' she murmured, making sure her body was an appropriate distance from Sam's so no one could say anything inappropriate was happening.

He twirled her again, both hands catching her at the waist as she spun back to face him and their eyes met. Eliza felt the desire ripple between them and she knew if it had been just the two of them she wouldn't have been able to resist swaying in closer and kissing Sam one more time.

By the anguished expression on his face, she suspected Sam was thinking the same, and she felt his fingers grip her a little harder.

It took all her self-control to push herself away from Sam and return to holding his arm as if she wasn't thinking thoughts no innocent debutante should.

They skated back to the busier part of the canal and joined the other groups of skaters moving steadily across the ice.

'What if neither of us falls?' Sam said as they nodded in greeting to another couple. 'What of the masquerade then?'

'I have to warn you I am completely and utterly ruthless,' Eliza said, flashing a mischievous smile in his direction. 'I am not above giving you a little push as you help me up the bank after we finish skating.'

'I do not believe it of you.'

'To get to the masquerade I would do it.'

'Hmm, I am too much of a gentleman to retaliate, of course, but I may insist on leaving the ice first, just to ensure I can help you better on to the bank, you understand.'

Eliza laughed and as soon as the sound left her mouth she knew it was too loud. No one in London seemed to want to express their true feelings and it meant spontaneous bursts of laughter were rarely heard. Even the most amusing of jokes was received with a polite titter.

'Shh,' Sam cautioned her. 'It is going to be hard enough to make people believe you will want to break off our engagement without them realising I am the most amusing man in London as well as the most eligible.'

'You'll never be able to show your face in the ballrooms of London again. The young women will find you completely irresistible—charming, amusing, and recently heartbroken and needing love and care to heal.'

Sam let out a groan. 'You're right. I think I will hide in the country for a year once this is over.'

'They might hunt you down, convinced they are the one to mend your damaged heart.'

He shuddered at her words and although it was in jest, Eliza wondered what it must be like for him, being pursued by the unmarried young ladies eager to have their chance with a wealthy and handsome bachelor.

'Some men would revel in it,' she murmured, 'but not you.'

'What was that?'

'I was wondering what it is like to be so eligible, so in demand from the debutantes and the other women who would wish to ensnare you.'

'Horrible,' he said shortly and then shook his head when he saw her expression. 'None of them know me and most of them don't care about getting to know me.'

'You aren't the most approachable.'

'Yet for some reason they still wish to marry me. I feel as though it is a transaction, reduced to what they see my worth in the world is.'

'At least they deem your worth high.'

'I know, and sometimes it feels ungrateful to feel that way, but I know all they see is the money and the hundreds upon hundreds of acres I own, the yearly income, the farms and estates across the country. They don't see me.'

Eliza paused, waiting for him to stop and look at her before speaking. 'I see you, Sam.'

For a long moment neither of them moved and Eliza felt as though the whole world was shifting underneath her. She had the urge to reach out and pull Sam towards her and damn the consequences.

The moment was broken by a deep, low crack that every ice skater dreaded. It wasn't underneath them but farther down the canal, but Eliza felt the tremor of the movement as the ice shifted.

'Quick,' Sam said, pulling her towards the bank and hoisting her unceremoniously on to dry land all within seconds. Eliza knew how treacherous ice could be and one little crack could soon turn to disaster. Holding her hand out to pull Sam up, she watched as he turned to survey the scene and knew immediately he wouldn't be joining her. 'I'll be back. Whatever happens, stay up there,' he said, and then was off across the ice.

Eliza fumbled with the knots that held her skates on, taking twice as long with stiff fingers even inside her gloves. She desperately needed to see what was happening, but knew she would be too encumbered by the skates to move fast enough on land. Eventually she managed to kick off the skates, grab them with one hand and then hurry along the bank.

Out on the ice she could see two young men frozen in place, both too scared to move. Standing a few feet farther back was Sam. All the other skaters had quickly dashed from the ice and were gathered with the crowd of onlookers, anxiously watching events unfold.

'Very slowly you need to skate towards me, Mr Farthington,' Sam said to the man closest to them. Eliza squinted and realised it was a young man she knew from her time spent at Lady Mountjoy's before they had come to London for the Season. He looked pale and nervous, and Eliza could see he was about to panic and do something stupid. 'No sudden moves, just one foot in front of the other, very calmly and slowly.'

'What about me?' the second man said. Eliza didn't think she recognised him, but heard the note of terror in his voice. Everyone knew plunging through cracked ice was extremely dangerous. She had even heard tales of people's hearts stopping on exposure to the icy water

and if you survived there was the very real chance of
lung congestion and fever if you swallowed any of the
dirty water.

'Once Mr Farthington has moved away there will be
less weight on the ice and we'll have you on dry land
in no time at all.'

'I can't move,' Mr Farthington stammered, his hands
reaching out and grasping at the air.

'Yes, you can,' Sam said, his voice so calm he could
be discussing the weather with a friend on a pleasant
spring day. 'Just slide one foot forward and then the
other.'

Eliza could hear him murmuring encouraging words
as Mr Farthington slowly began moving. She felt her
pulse quicken as there was another ominous crack and
she wished she could call out, to beg Sam to come back
to the bank, back to safety, but she knew he wouldn't
leave while the other two men were still in danger.

It seemed to take for ever for Mr Farthington to reach
Sam, who gave him a reassuring squeeze on the arm
and then directed him to keep going to the bank. When
he was on solid ground he looked around, startled, as
if he had been unaware of all the concerned onlookers.
As his eyes met Eliza's, Mr Farthington gave a shaky
smile and a nod of greeting in recognition of the time
they had spent as part of the same party at Lady Mountjoy's country estate in the summer, before moving away
and collapsing in relief on to a nearby bench to watch
the scene unfolding on the ice.

Eliza could see Sam's eyes were now locked on the

man in front of him and she gasped as she saw a frac-
ture in the ice appearing between Sam and the man.

'You need to move now,' Sam said, his voice not be-
traying the panic he must feel.

'If I move, the ice will crack.'

'Move quickly, lunge towards me and I will catch
you if it cracks.'

'I'll be trapped in the water.'

'I promise I will not let that happen.'

The man gave a shaky nod and took a deep breath,
lunging forward just as there was an even louder crack
and the ice beneath him started to splinter, falling into
the water in jagged pieces. Sam grabbed hold of the
man's arms and pulled him across the ice, both of them
tumbling on to their backs and sliding away from the
area that had cracked, hitting the bank where there were
half a dozen hands ready to pull them up.

Eliza couldn't help herself. As Sam was pulled on
to the bank, she ran at him and threw her arms around
his neck, burying her face in his chest.

She couldn't find the words to express how worried
she had been, instead squeezing him tight to her.

'Hush,' Sam said, 'nothing happened.' She thought
he might pry her away, always vigilant of how other
people might be looking at them, but instead he looped
an arm around her waist and held her tightly.

'Thank you.' A shaky voice came from behind them.
It was the man they had saved from the ice, looking pale
and drawn, but otherwise unharmed. 'I can't believe I
froze out there. If you hadn't been there…'

'You would have been fine,' Sam said, giving the

man a pat on the arm. 'I suggest you get home to warm up and have a large brandy.'

'I will. Thank you.'

As the man walked away, Sam gently extracted himself from Eliza's grip and she turned to see the eyes of the crowd that had gathered upon them.

'We're not doing well at remaining inconspicuous, are we?' Sam murmured in her ear, and Eliza had to suppress a smile.

Chapter Thirteen

'I need to talk to you both. Right now,' Lady Mount-joy said, looking ruffled as she took hold of Sam's and Eliza's arms and guided them into the drawing room, shutting the door firmly behind her.

'Good evening,' Sam said, giving his most affable smile. Eliza had to stop herself from giggling, knowing he was being overly polite to try to dampen down some of the agitation Lady Mountjoy was displaying.

'Tell me,' Lady Mountjoy said, not distracted by Sam's polite greeting, 'what on earth were you both thinking?'

Eliza opened her mouth to begin answering, but Lady Mountjoy held up her hand in a way that made Eliza realise she didn't really want an answer, at least not yet.

'You tell me that you do not want to be forced to marry, that this engagement is a bind, a chore for both of you. Then, not two weeks later, you go cavorting around London unchaperoned, dancing on the ice to an audience of dozens if not hundreds of interested eyes and

embracing on the banks of the canal in St James's Park.'
Lady Mountjoy took a steadying breath. 'The drawing
rooms are filled with gossip and speculation with everyone saying they've never seen a young couple so in
love. They are all invested in your story, your journey
together and they cannot wait to see what happens next.'

Eliza risked a glance at Sam, wondering whether
this would send him running for his country estate. If
anything, he looked relaxed, unperturbed by this turn
of events.

'I do not have to tell you what this means. Any hope
of quietly drifting apart has been dashed. There will
not be a scandal big enough to take the glare of attention from you two.'

Eliza nodded. She was realising things might not
work out as she had once hoped. Initially, when Lady
Mountjoy had discussed the plan of the fake engagement, Eliza had thought it would be a few weeks of pretending, and then she and Sam would go their separate
ways, with people not caring about the fate of an insignificant young woman from Somerset. Now it was becoming apparent she would not be able to break off the
engagement without an ensuing scandal. She would be
tainted—either the young woman thrown over by Lord
Thannock, or the young woman foolish enough to walk
away from London's most eligible bachelor.

'You still have options, Eliza,' Sam said, smiling at
her reassuringly.

'Of course you do,' Lady Mountjoy said, softening
a little. 'You can marry, of course, find another suitor
who will take your hand. Or you can return to Somer-

set. I doubt too many people there will care what has happened in London.'

'There is a third option,' Sam said slowly, and for a moment Eliza thought he was going to suggest they make their pretend engagement real. She was surprised to feel her heart pounding in her chest and the thrum of anticipation rush through her body. It wasn't what she had wanted to begin with, but after spending these few weeks with Sam it wouldn't be the terrible prospect she had first thought. 'I could do something awful, something that would justify your breaking off our engagement.'

Eliza quickly shook her head. 'No. I will not ask you to do that for me.' The idea made her feel sick in her stomach and she hoped he would quickly forget it. She felt foolish for wondering if he might actually want to marry her, that he might ask her to be his wife for real, but more than foolish when she realised she was disappointed. It had never been part of the plan, never been part of their bargain, but for a moment she had felt that flare of hope before it had been dashed by his practical solution.

'At least think about it, Eliza. You don't want to marry and you don't want to return to Somerset. This may allow you to escape judgement and enjoy the rest of your Season.'

'By sacrificing you. No, I won't do that.'

Sam smiled at her, a smile that made her heart soar despite the serious subject they were discussing.

'You know it will not be lasting for me. I can hide away in the country for a few months, pretend to lick my wounds and then make my return to London. I'll still be wealthy, I'll still be titled, and I'll still be eligible.'

'No Sam, you've already done enough for me. More than enough.'

'Perhaps take some time to think about it,' Lady Mountjoy said, eyeing Sam with interest.

She stood, patting then both on the hand, and then turned to leave.

'Carriages will be ready in five minutes,' she said, walking out into the hall. 'Don't forget your masks.'

For a long moment they sat in silence, both contemplating the conversation they had just been a part of.

'You're trying to become an actual saint, aren't you?' Eliza said in a low whisper.

'Only three good deeds away from sainthood.'

'Thank you for agreeing to come to the masquerade tonight.'

He inclined his head. 'Although if anyone I know, badly disguised in a tiny mask, approaches me and pretends to be a stranger, I am leaving immediately.'

'Duly noted, and not entirely unreasonable.'

They were interrupted by Miss Huntley sweeping down the stairs, her normally icy demeanour breaking into a warm smile when she saw Lord Thannock was visiting. Eliza rolled her eyes and marvelled at how charming the sarcastic young woman could be when she tried.

'How wonderful to see you, Lord Thannock,' she gushed, walking over and touching Sam fleetingly on the arm. 'What a treat to have you accompany us to the masquerade.'

Sam smiled, but refrained from telling Miss Huntley his true thoughts on masquerades.

'Perhaps some of your friends might be in attendance?'

'If they are, I will be sure to introduce you, Miss Huntley.'

'You are too kind, Lord Thannock. We all owe you so much.' With a flick of her fan, Miss Huntley moved on, leaving Eliza to roll her eyes at the young woman's back and Sam to stifle a laugh at her behaviour.

'Lord Thannock, how delightful it is to have you attend,' Mrs Willingham gushed as it was their turn to greet their hosts at the door. 'Miss Stanley, you must share your secret. I have been inviting Lord Thannock to my ball for years—I think this year I feel your influence in his decision to attend?'

'Lord Thannock knows I love to dance,' Eliza said, smiling beatifically up at her pretend fiancé, 'I merely mentioned my desire to attend your ball and he made it happen.'

Mrs Willingham leaned in a little closer. '*All* the ladies of my circle are very eager to hear how you and Lord Thannock fell in love.'

Eliza searched the older woman's face for signs that she was being rude in an underhand way, saying Eliza and Sam did not belong together, but there was only honest interest in her expression.

'It was a whirlwind,' Sam said, inclining his head to their hostess and then gripping Eliza by the arm and quickly moving on.

'Mrs Willingham will not be the last person to question you tonight,' Lady Mountjoy said as they entered the ballroom. It was a beautiful room, decorated in pale green and gold, the light colours giving the room an airy feel.

Next to her, Eliza heard Sam groan.

'You may groan, Samuel, as long as you have your answers straight. You will not be together all of the evening and you can be certain some people will be comparing your stories when you are apart.'

Eliza felt a jolt of panic. She and Sam had a basic story worked out, but not the details. Grimacing, she looked up at the man beside her. They were so different, complete opposites, it wouldn't be enough to simply hope they would come up with ideas and stories that roughly matched.

'Stop worrying,' Sam said. 'Be vague, change the subject, walk away if you have to.'

'You have no idea how women's conversations with each other work, do you?'

He fixed her with a dubious stare.

'Someone will corner me and suggest we go for a stroll around the ballroom. Before I can refuse they will have taken my arm and we will be promenading and it will be too late to escape because any hurried exit will be inexplicably rude. Then the woman will start to drop hints that she knows some salacious detail about our lives and will press and press and press until I reveal something I really shouldn't.'

Even with the mask covering his face, Eliza knew the exact expression he was wearing.

'It is different for you,' she muttered.

'Only because I make it different.'

'No, women are too eager to make a good impression on you to risk your displeasure with that sort of questioning and men are less likely to be interested at all.'

'Remember, tonight you cease to be Miss Eliza Stanley, instead you are the mysterious woman in the gold-feathered mask.'

Eliza snorted with laughter, a sound that earned her an admonishing look from Lady Mountjoy. Quickly, she covered her lips with her hand as she regained her composure.

'As you said, there is not a single person in the room who does not know who you and I are tonight, with or without the masks.'

Lady Mountjoy ushered Lucy, Jane and Miss Huntley ahead of her and then turned to face Eliza and Sam.

'Please remember everyone is watching you tonight,' she said quietly. 'Everything you do is going to be judged. Use it to your advantage, use tonight to create the story you want people to believe.'

Eliza nodded, wondering exactly what she wanted people to believe.

'Another evening playing the part of the lovesick suitor,' Sam grumbled, but Eliza could see he wasn't really all that put out. It was the whole reason he had agreed to come after all.

'And you should talk and dance with other gentlemen, let it be seen this isn't the fairy tale it is being built up to be. We need some room to manoeuvre, some room to let other suitors in,' Lady Mountjoy said.

Eliza nodded, feeling slightly numb. *This* was what she had come to London for, the excitement and spectacle of a ball, a masquerade no less. For years she had dreamed of this, dreamed of sparkling ballrooms, ladies in beautiful dresses, gentlemen in finely tailored evening jackets, the music, the laughter, the joy. It had been what she had wanted over all else, even though it had been hard to imagine in her little bedroom in Somerset.

In front of her Lucy and Jane were gesturing for her to join them as they moved farther into the ballroom, but for a moment Eliza hesitated.

'Go,' Sam said, giving her a smile that she knew he hardly ever bestowed on anyone else. 'Enjoy. I will find you for the third dance.'

She stepped away, feeling strange deep inside, as if part of her were hollow. She had the urge to turn back to Sam, to ask him to dance with her now, to spend the evening by his side, but when she turned around he had gone, melted into the crush of people.

Eliza forced herself to turn back and plunge into the crowds of the ballroom. She caught Lucy's hand and was pulled in even deeper and as the music swelled she felt some of her usual determination to enjoy every last moment of the masquerade.

It felt as though she were in a dream as they darted through the ballroom. Some people were wearing simple black or coloured masks that only covered their eyes, but most people had embraced the spirit of the masquerade and had elaborate costumes and masks to complement them.

One man was dressed as a stag, with huge golden

antlers on his head. His companion, a petite woman with beautiful green eyes behind her mask, was dressed as a peacock. The mask that covered the top part of her face was a brilliant blue, as was her dress, and she had row upon row of peacock feathers attached to her collar and hair.

Unable to tear her eyes away from the peacock costume, Eliza bumped into someone, and as she turned she felt her eyes widen as she came face to face with a woman in an exquisite dress covered in hieroglyphics. Eliza wondered at the sheer extravagance of the outfit as it must have been custom made for the ball with each symbol sewn into the fabric in gold thread. It was hardly a dress that could easily be worn again.

'Lucy, this is incredible,' Eliza said, squeezing her friend's hand. She glanced down at her own dress, beautiful sky-blue fabric with shimmery silver threads pulled through. Lady Mountjoy had insisted they all have new gowns for the masquerade and the four debutantes all had dresses that were meant to represent the sky at different times of day. Jane had opted for an inky blue with hundreds of tiny golden stars embroidered from neckline to hem on one side. Lucy had chosen a beautiful silver and grey gown that looked like a moody autumn's sky and Miss Huntley had searched for the right material for a long time before deciding on a luxurious golden fabric that reflected the light and shone like the sun itself.

As she followed Lucy's path through the crowd, Eliza couldn't keep the smile from her face. This masquerade was even more spectacular than she had ever imagined.

* * *

Sam was on his best behaviour this evening. He had danced once with an insipid young woman he barely knew and had even made small talk with countless guests he really would have rather avoided.

None of this commanded his entire attention, though. One eye was always fixed on Eliza, aware of where she was in the ballroom at any given moment. He knew when she laughed for ten minutes with the charming Mr Hautby and when she struggled to extricate herself from the less desirable Mr Williams. He knew when she danced and even when she enjoyed it and when she didn't.

It disconcerted him when she was guided out on to the terrace by the notorious Lord Johnson and he was already halfway to the door when she dashed back through it, her eyes catching his and giving him a reassuring smile.

Tonight Eliza sparkled. Her dress was made of a shimmery light blue material with threads of silver pulled through. In her hair she wore a delicate crystal clip. Sam knew it was glass or paste, but it shone enough to make the unknowing wonder if it was diamond. It wasn't just her clothes, though—Eliza herself sparkled. Every time he caught a glimpse of her face he saw her smile, her eyes alight with the excitement of the evening. She looked radiant and happy.

Unexpectedly Sam felt as though he had been punched in the gut and quickly had to excuse himself from a dull conversation about the fashions of the Season and make his way for the doors to the terrace. Once he was outside he took deep gulps of air until things felt a little more normal.

Shaking his head, he tried to dismiss the disappointment he'd felt when he had seen Eliza smiling and dancing and *thriving* in the ballroom. This was her world, the life she had always wanted. He couldn't ever ask her to give it up.

'You don't want her,' he muttered, reminding himself of all the reasons they would make a terrible couple. Rationally, he knew they were all true, but it didn't stop the irrational part of him wanting her.

'Lord Thannock?' It was Eliza's voice, quiet but familiar in the evening air.

She was calling him from the door to the ballroom and peering out into the darkness, unsure if he was there.

'I'm here,' he said, stepping forward.

'I saw you leave...' She paused before continuing, 'You didn't look well.'

He wondered if she had been watching him the way he had been watching her.

'I'm fine.'

'My mother never lets us use that word,' Eliza said with a smile, taking a step out into the darkness.

'It is a little bland.'

'You can hide so much behind it. Is something amiss?'

'No. I'm not good with these occasions.'

'You are the toast of the ball. Everywhere I go there are huddles of people talking about you, discussing what a fine figure you cut in your evening jacket, marvelling at how charming you are being this evening.'

'Hmm.'

'Honestly, they are.'

'I believe you. I just wish they wouldn't. You look as though you've been enjoying yourself.'

'Oh, yes, it has been lovely.' She looked up at him and he saw the sparkle in her eyes. 'Thank you for agreeing to come.'

'It's my pleasure, Eliza.' He almost added he liked to see her happy, but stopped himself. They had already agreed they could not go down that path and out here, with just the low glow of candlelight from the ballroom, it would be so easy to pull Eliza to him, take her in his arms and lose himself in her kiss.

'Our dance will be starting soon,' Eliza said.

'Yes, of course.'

'We don't have to go back inside for it if you don't want.'

He had an image of them dancing on the terrace, just the two of them. He would be able to hold her closer, caress her body through her dress.

Clearing his throat, he shook his head. 'We should return to the ballroom. It only takes one person to notice we have gone and the rumours will start again.'

Eliza nodded, but made no attempt to move. 'What you said earlier, about doing something that will allow me to break away from you and continue with the Season?'

Sam waited for her to continue, wondering if she was going to accept his offer.

'I don't want you to do that,' she said, looking up at him with her deep green eyes. 'Promise me you won't.'

'It may be the best way, Eliza.'

'Promise me. Please.'

Sam took a step towards her and then another until they were standing just inches apart. He could see her breathing deepen and her tongue darted out to wet her lips. The urge to kiss her was overwhelming and Sam could think of nothing else but pulling her into his arms.

'Eliza,' he murmured. 'I can't promise that.' He reached out and held her by the waist, and ever so slowly, Eliza took a final step towards him. Their bodies were touching and Sam knew if anyone came out of the ballroom now their plan was ruined for sure. They would have to marry or Eliza would be ruined. Even this thought couldn't stop him and without any more delay he kissed her.

He'd meant to be gentle, but as his lips brushed against Eliza's, Sam let out a groan and kissed her deeply. Eliza responded, looping her arms around his neck and kissing him hard. She tasted sweet, like the lemonade she must have been drinking, and Sam knew he could kiss her for hours.

Together they stumbled back a little until Eliza was pressed up against the wall and Sam's hands started to move over her body. He loved the way she pressed against him, responding to his touch, and for a moment he forgot where they were and that only a few feet away through the door to the ballroom were a hundred people who would judge their actions immediately.

With his fingers trailing along the neckline of her dress, Sam was about to push it down when a loud voice from just beyond the door made him stiffen and freeze.

'Mr Peters…yes, it is hot, isn't it? Were you on your way to get some air?' He recognised it as Eliza's friend Lucy Freeman's voice, and with it he and Eliza immediately sprang apart.

For a moment they just looked at one another. Both were dishevelled and it was obvious what they had been doing.

The door from the terrace opened and Miss Jane Ashworth, the other of Eliza's friends, slipped out.

'Oh, my,' she exclaimed as she saw them. It took her a moment to take in the scene in front of her before she was able to recover enough to spring into action. Quickly, she straightened Eliza's dress and smoothed her hair as beyond the door they heard Miss Freeman trying to stall Mr Peters for a bit longer. 'Take my arm,' Miss Ashworth whispered to Eliza. 'Lord Thannock, fall into step with us, but a few feet away. This way it looks as though you were never unchaperoned.'

Sam was still straightening his cravat as the door from the ballroom opened and Mr Peters and another man Sam did not recognise stepped out.

'Good evening,' Sam said, nodding to the two men, thankful when they didn't seem overly interested in their little group.

'It must be nearly time for the third dance,' Miss Ashworth said cheerily. 'Perhaps, Eliza, we might have time to freshen ourselves up before you rejoin Lord Thannock.'

'Yes,' Eliza said, her voice a little shaky. 'That sounds like a good idea.'

Sam let them go first, seeing the flick of Miss Freeman's dress as she joined her friends, taking Eliza's arm on the other side to hurry her through the ballroom.

Not wanting to get drawn into conversation with Mr Peters and his companion, Sam moved to the door, checking himself over in the blurry reflection in the glass before he stepped back into the ballroom.

Thankfully, no one seemed to be paying him any attention and there certainly weren't any interested looks or whispered words as he reappeared.

He stalked around the perimeter of the ballroom, making his way to where drinks were being served. He eschewed the punch, far too sweet for his tastes, and took a glass of wine instead.

As he turned back to survey the ballroom, his heart sank. Even with a mask over her eyes he would recognise his mother anywhere. She was dressed flamboyantly as usual in a dress that had ancient Grecian tones and a wreath of flowers in her hair.

'Sam, darling, I've been keeping an eye on you,' she slurred, and Sam felt the familiar dread he often did when encountering his mother at events. In the past few years he had worked hard to ensure it didn't happen too frequently, but when he had been younger, back in London fresh from a term at Oxford, he had often found his mother at the heart of the social events he had attended.

Sometimes it hadn't been a problem. He would check she was able to look after herself and then quietly leave, but other times she was barely able to stand let alone look after herself. His friends were sympathetic and many times had helped him find her a carriage home or ensured the way was smoothed.

For a long time Sam had worried about her, worried she would be taken advantage of or fall in front of a moving carriage, but over the years he had seen how resilient his mother was, even with half a bottle of gin inside her.

He hadn't even known she was coming tonight. For the past couple of days she had been staying with an old friend and they must have decided to attend together.

'Do you need me to arrange a carriage for you?'

'Nonsense. The night is young. There are hours and hours until the ball ends yet.'

She stumbled a little, and instinctively Sam reached out to steady her.

'My good boy,' she murmured as he looped an arm around her waist to steady her. 'You're too good for that little conniving social climber.'

'I know you have had too much to drink, but please do not speak of Miss Stanley that way,' he said coldly.

'She's pretty, but what else is there? You should be marrying the daughter of an earl or a duke or a marquess.'

'It is none of your concern what I do,' he said, peering at her to see how much she had likely had to drink that evening. If it was just a couple of glasses, he could make his escape and find Eliza, but if it was more, then he would need to ensure his mother was safely on her way home first.

Carefully, he let her go, seeing if she could stand by herself. For a moment she stayed still, but then swayed slightly and stumbled. With a loud exhalation of breath, Sam looked around to see if Eliza was back in the ballroom yet. He needed to see her, to talk to her. This was the worst possible moment for him to be disappearing.

'We should talk about Eliza,' he said, lowering his voice to his mother. 'I have a proposition.'

'Go on.'

'If you agree to go home without any fuss and sleep off whatever it is you have imbibed tonight, I will listen to your concerns about Eliza and we shall discuss matters fully tomorrow.'

His mother reached up and patted him on the cheek as if he were still a little boy.

'You're a good boy, Samuel. Always looking out for your mother.'

'Come on. I will arrange a carriage. How did you get here?'

'I came with Lady Penelope Killman.' Lady Killman was one of his mother's few remaining friends. Over the years she had insulted or embarrassed too many friends to receive many invitations.

Sam chewed his lip and then made a decision. Lady Mountjoy had always told him no favour was ever too big to ask. She would not mind if he used one of her carriages to send his mother home. It could then circle back in plenty of time to be there for when Lady Mountjoy or any of their party wanted to leave.

Quickly, he arranged the transport and after ten minutes his mother was safely closeted inside the carriage.

'Goodnight,' he called as it pulled away, wondering what it would be like to have a parent who acted responsibly.

Rubbing his temples, he returned to the ballroom

to see the dance he had promised to Eliza had already started. By the looks of it the couples had been dancing for a good few minutes. His eyes darted around the ballroom, trying to find Eliza. He needed to talk to her, needed to explain. Even if he had no idea what he might say to her.

She wasn't among the group of young ladies gathered near the edge of the dance floor, no doubt strategically placed to catch a gentleman's eye and encourage him to ask them to dance. She wasn't in the crowd at the far end of the ballroom, or on the chairs set around the edge.

He caught sight of her two friends, both standing alongside Lady Mountjoy, and started to make his way through the ballroom.

With a nod of greeting he shot an enquiring look at Miss Freeman and Miss Ashworth.

'There you are,' Lady Mountjoy said before either of the young women could answer him. 'Where on earth did you get to? Miss Stanley was looking for you for your dance.'

'My mother. She was stumbling around. I hope you don't mind, but I've sent her home in your carriage as I didn't bring mine. The driver knows to come back immediately afterwards.'

'Of course not,' Lady Mountjoy said, giving him a warm smile.

'Where is Miss Stanley now?'

'She agreed to dance with Mr Hautby again. He was quite persuasive.' Lady Mountjoy fixed him with a determined smile. 'I think he has taken a liking to her.'

'Oh, good,' Sam said without feeling, already excusing himself and making his way towards the dance floor.

He hadn't seen her before, but now he did, tucked away at the edge with Mr Hautby, their position showing they were probably a minute late in joining the dance. Even so Mr Hautby looked suitably pleased and Eliza was managing to smile and make conversation.

Sam knew the moment she caught sight of him. Something changed in her posture. Still, her eyes remained fixed on her partner, but Sam knew she was working hard not to look at him.

He tried not to glower every time Mr Hautby turned in his direction, but it was hard to do. It would only take a few seconds to apologise to Eliza—she was a reasonable woman and as soon as she heard it was dealing with his mother that had delayed him she would forgive him. Right now she would be hurt and confused and wondering why he had abandoned her after kissing her so passionately.

It was clear the dance wasn't ending any time soon, so Sam forced himself to take a step back. He needed to work out what he was going to say to Eliza when he finally was able to get her alone, or as alone as they would be able to be with the ears of the ballroom listening in.

She hadn't wanted his apology the first time he had kissed her, but he owed her one this time. After everything they had agreed, everything they had said, he hadn't been able to show some simple restraint.

Sam didn't blame himself for wanting to kiss Eliza. There was an overwhelming attraction between them, a desire unlike anything he had ever known before. *That* was something outside of his control, something made deep in his subconscious. What he could control, what he *should* be able to control, was how he acted. He had acknowledged his desire for Eliza—the least he could do now was stop himself from kissing her any time there was even a hint of privacy.

As he watched the couples dance and parade across the dance floor, allowing himself to be mesmerised by the colour and movement of the dresses and the steps all in unison, he tried to ask himself what he really wanted with Eliza.

There was the attraction, that was undeniable. Then there was the friendship, something he had never expected to build between him and the headstrong young woman he had initially thought to be foolish.

'Nothing more,' he muttered. There could not be anything more. He had watched her sparkle and come to life at the masquerade this evening. He couldn't give her this. He wanted something so completely different it would pull them apart and make them both miserable.

He would apologise, acknowledge the attraction and then promise her it would never happen again. In a few more weeks they would have gone their separate ways, one way or another, and he would just have to learn to let her go.

The dance seemed to last for ever and every time the music swelled he thought it was coming to an end, poised to step forward and claim his fake fiancée before anyone else could.

After another long few minutes it finally finished and the couples smiled breathlessly at each other, lingering to talk, to discuss the dance and laugh at their missteps.

'Miss Stanley,' he called, not too loudly, but enough to grab the attention of the people around him.

Eliza turned slowly and regarded him, a polite smile on her face. She took her time thanking Mr Hautby for the dance before she made her way through the crowd to his side.

Chapter Fourteen

Eliza was still breathless as she stopped a few paces in front of Sam, regarding his pained expression and wondering if it really was that terrible to kiss her. Once she had been whisked away by Jane and Lucy she had been barely able to think, let alone speak. Thankfully her friends were more concerned no one else saw anything was amiss than pressing her for details. It had taken a few minutes to tidy her appearance and then she had returned to the ballroom, ready for her dance with Sam.

It had hurt more than it should when he had abandoned her.

'You weren't there,' Eliza said quietly.

'I'm sorry. I went to get a drink and I was cornered by my mother.' Eliza started to interrupt him, but Sam quickly pushed on. 'She had been drinking far too much for far too long—I had to arrange for her to get home in a carriage.'

Eliza felt some of the anger fizzle and then burn out, knowing Sam wouldn't have chosen to spend time with his mother under any circumstance.

'I'm sorry I missed our dance.'

'Mr Hautby was happy to step in.'

'I could see. Will you dance the fourth with me?'

She knew it would be petty to say no and, more than anything, she wanted to feel Sam's hands on her again, even if it was in the chaste context of a dance.

'Yes, of course.'

'And then perhaps we can find somewhere a little quieter to talk.'

'Quieter, but not secluded. It was only because of Lucy and Jane we weren't caught.'

'I must thank your friends,' Sam murmured.

Eliza looked up at him, trying to read his expression. It was no time at all ago that he had been apologising for kissing her when they were sat at the piano and now they had done it again. She wondered what he wanted to say to her and realised part of her didn't want to know. She didn't want him to tell her they needed to spend time apart, to overcome this desire that surged between them. Equally, she didn't want him to think he had to propose for real because they had almost got caught kissing for a second time.

'What do you want?' she murmured under her breath. The question was directed at herself, but Sam gave her an appraising look as if he were thinking the same thing.

There was only time to find a quick glass of lemonade before the music signalling the next dance started, and Eliza took her place on the dance floor. Of course it had to be a waltz, the first of the evening. All the other dances had been livelier with less contact and less time being held close, able to do nothing but stare into your partner's eyes.

Sam held out his hand and Eliza placed her fingers in his palm. Taking a deep, steadying breath, she looked up.

As the music swelled they began, stepping and twirling with the other couples, but for Eliza it was as if they all faded into the background. It felt as though they were the only two in the room, their eyes locked on one another's, everything about them synchronised and in tune.

'Thank you for the dance,' Sam said, his voice low. Eliza could see he had been equally affected and for a long moment they both stood on the dance floor while the other couples moved away around them. 'We should find somewhere to talk,' Sam repeated, finally breaking away.

'Yes. Perhaps I will go and sit on the chairs by the refreshment table. No one else is there at the moment. If you fetch me a glass of lemonade, we can then sit and talk while I pretend I am pausing for a refreshment.'

'Good idea.'

On Sam's arm, Eliza weaved through the crowded ballroom, catching Lucy's eye as they went past where her friend was standing, but giving a minuscule shake of her head to show she was not going to do anything foolish.

Once she was comfortably seated at the edge of the ballroom and Sam had returned with a glass of lemonade, she turned towards him.

Sam was sitting next to her, looking out at the ballroom full of people.

'They all think we're engaged,' he murmured. For one crazy moment, Eliza thought he was going to say why didn't they just get married for real. She felt her heart skip in her chest and the roil of nerves in her belly, but Sam didn't turn to her and ask the question. Eliza closed her eyes, trying to block out the pain of rejection. She couldn't keep thinking Sam was going to propose to her, it was too difficult to bear when it didn't happen. Twice now she had thought he was going to suggest they do away with their deception and give in to the attraction between them and neither time had anything come of it.

Sam exhaled loudly and shook his head. 'I don't think we should allow ourselves to be alone together,' he said with a rueful smile.

Eliza was surprised at the disappointment that washed over her as he shook his head at the memory of their behaviour. She stayed silent, hoping her face wasn't showing all the emotions that were fighting for supremacy inside.

'Sam,' she said so quietly she knew he would have to lean in to hear her. 'How do you feel about me?'

She watched him as he thought about the question, saw the flare of alarm in his eyes and wondered if he was worried about hurting her feelings or worried he might reveal too many of his own feelings.

'That's a big question, Eliza.'

'I know.'

For a moment he sat in silence and just as he was opening his mouth to speak there was a commotion in the crowd and they saw Lady Mountjoy hurrying towards them.

'Lord Thannock, you are needed in the drawing room.'

Sam stood immediately, but didn't move away, waiting for Lady Mountjoy to explain what was so urgent.

In a quieter voice Lady Mountjoy continued. 'Your mother must have instructed the driver to turn around and she returned to the ball where she has continued to drink. She is in the drawing room, but I think you need to ensure she gets home. Soon.'

Eliza watched as the colour drained from Sam's face and his frown deepened. Without even looking back, he started through the ballroom and Eliza stood to follow.

'It may be best to let Sam deal with this on his own, dear,' Lady Mountjoy said, smiling at her reassuringly. 'His mother can have a cruel tongue when she is inebriated.'

For a moment, Eliza paused, but then decided to follow Sam anyway. She would stay back, keep out of his mother's line of sight, but would be there to offer any support Sam might need.

In the drawing room there was an awkward sort of hush. People were obviously watching the scene unfold between mother and son, but good manners meant they didn't want to stare openly. This meant conversations were continuing, but there were long pauses as the onlookers were distracted by the events at one end of the room.

'Did you win anything?' Sam was asking his mother. His voice was calm and his expression looked genuinely interested.

'No, they're all scoundrels and cheats here,' Lady Thannock slurred.

'Don't let them hear you say that. You won't be welcome at the tables again,' Sam said conspiratorially.

For a minute he merely sat with his mother, passing comment on what was happening in the room, and Eliza couldn't work out what was going on. Then it slowly dawned on her that Sam must have had a lot of experience in removing his mother from potentially embarrassing situations when she was drunk.

She watched as he tilted his head towards his mother and spoke quietly. 'The ball is winding down and it has been a little dull if I am honest. Shall we make our escape and find that special bottle of brandy I've been saving back home?'

Eliza found she was holding her breath until his mother nodded and started to struggle to her feet.

'Never liked masquerades,' she heard the older woman mumble.

'I know, strange idea all dressing up in masks when everyone knows who everyone else is anyway,' Sam said, taking his mother's arm to steady her. Even with him taking her weight the older woman stumbled and weaved, her eyes unfocused as she walked.

'Can I help?' Eliza said, stepping forward, not wanting to aggravate the situation, but seeing that Lady Thannock might break free and take a tumble at any moment.

For an instant Sam's eyes widened as he waited for his mother's reaction, but either she was too drunk to recognise Eliza or too far gone to care as she held out her free arm and let Eliza grip it and take some of her weight.

Lady Mountjoy strode ahead, clearing the way and quickly encouraging the footmen to arrange for the carriage to be brought to the bottom of the steps.

Lady Thannock was about to step up into the carriage when she turned back and looked at the house.

'I don't know if I want to leave actually, Samuel,' she said, taking a step back towards the front door.

Eliza caught the look of alarm on Sam's face and wondered how she could help, but Lady Mountjoy got there first.

'The ball is almost over,' she said, leaning in to Lady Thannock and whispering in a conspiratorial fashion, 'and it wasn't all that lively to begin with. We shall accompany you and then the carriage can return us home after.'

This seemed to placate Lady Thannock, and Sam gave Lady Mountjoy a look of gratitude over his mother's head.

It took a few minutes to bustle everyone into the awaiting carriage, for a footman to find Lady Mountjoy's cloak and Eliza's coat and to be instructed to inform Lord Mountjoy what had occurred and hand over the responsibility of seeing the other young women Lady Mountjoy was chaperoning home.

Much of the carriage ride was silent. Eliza was sitting next to Sam, their legs pressed together, and after a few minutes her hand sought his in the darkness and she entwined her fingers with his under the cover of a fold of her dress.

* * *

Lady Thannock was snoring quietly by the time they reached Sam's town house and he had to rouse her to manoeuvre her out of the carriage and into the house. Eliza and Lady Mountjoy followed them inside, settling in the warmth of the drawing room. A maid hurried in and saw to the fire and Eliza felt herself relaxing.

It had been a strange evening with an even stranger ending and she felt as though she had no idea where she stood with Sam. She knew him well enough to know that he would not abandon her in their ruse of an engagement, but she didn't know how he felt about her or even how she felt about him.

Eliza's eyes were drooping when she heard Sam re-enter the room and forced herself to stir.

'I've handed her over to the care of her lady's maid,' Sam said, running a hand through his hair before slumping into a chair a few feet away. 'I am assured she will be sleeping off her excesses soon.'

'I'm sorry, Sam,' Eliza said.

'It isn't your fault.'

'I know, but I'm still sorry you have to go through this.'

He nodded, and Eliza realised he looked exhausted with worry.

'Shall I take Lady Mountjoy home?'

They both looked across at the older woman who had nodded off in a chair by the fire. She was soundly asleep, her chest rising and falling slowly and evenly.

'In a minute. Would you like some fresh air first? I feel as if I need to clear my head.'

Eliza stood, stretching out her tired legs, and before following Sam wrapped herself in her coat, aware it would feel cold outside after being in such a wonderfully warm room.

'This is my favourite thing about this house,' Sam said as they stepped out of the back doors and into the garden. There was a small terrace area and then a long, narrow garden stretching back into the darkness. The moon was out and in the shadows Eliza could make out neat flower borders and stone statues. In the middle of the lawn was a bubbling fountain with a small pool underneath. 'My parents owned a slightly smaller house in Grosvenor Square, the heart of London my mother used to call it, but I never felt comfortable there and when I saw this house I knew this was where I wanted to be if I was in London.'

They strolled over to the fountain, and Eliza peered into the pool below. The water was clean and clear, but an inky black in the darkness. She perched on the edge of the stone rim of the pond, careful not to get any of her dress wet. Sam stood for a moment longer before sitting down beside her.

'What a night,' he said after a minute of silence.

'A good night or a bad night?'

'Some parts good,' he said, managing a smile. 'Some definitely not so good.'

'Your mother hasn't always been like this?'

'No…' he hesitated '…or at least I never knew. I was shielded from many of her antics as a child by the mere fact that she wasn't around much. I don't think she always used to get drunk, it isn't the impression I get when I talk to people she knew back then.' He shrugged. 'By all accounts she was very popular, someone everyone wanted at their events. You wouldn't feel that way about a woman who was inebriated and embarrassing, would you?'

'No.'

'She doesn't get many invitations now, only from those of a lower social rank desperate to climb a little higher or from good friends who still remember the person she was.'

'I can see why you find it easier when she is not here in London with you.'

'We're both happier. If we are not residing in the same city I do not have to know what she gets up to and she does not feel constrained by my expectations.'

'Was it the same for your father, do you think?'

A melancholy look passed over Sam's face, and Eliza regretted asking the question.

'In a way, I suppose. He loved her very much and used to swing between wanting to give her the freedom to do what she wanted and wanting to be part of her world.' Sam shook his head sadly. 'It didn't work.'

'What will you do now?'

He sighed and looked up at the house, to the bedrooms on the upper floors. 'She has a good friend in Scotland, someone who she has known since she was a girl. When things get bad I write to her and my mother goes to stay for a few months. It normally settles her down, resets things a little. Often she comes back healthy and happy and promising things will be different.'

'But they never are?'

'Not so far. Perhaps one day there will be a miracle.'

'You've written to this friend of your mother's?'

'I did as soon as my mother arrived from Europe. A year ago she wrote to say she had fallen in love and was planning to settle down with some Italian count. I have no idea what happened, but I think it ended in disaster. My mother needs time to heal without throwing herself back into society and hopefully without the drink.'

'I never knew you had such family worries, Sam, I'm sorry.'

'It is nothing compared to what some people have. At least mine is just one person.'

'One person who is meant to care for you, to be the one who looks out for you.'

In the darkness their eyes met, and Eliza felt the invisible pull. She wanted to reach out, to touch him, to comfort him, even though she knew they couldn't keep repeating the same mistake over and over again.

Quickly, she stood, needing to put some physical distance between herself and Sam.

'Sometimes I worry,' she said after a moment. 'All these dreams I had when I was in Somerset, I thought they would sustain me for ever.'

'Tell me.'

'I dreamed of ballrooms and grand houses and beautiful dresses. I dreamed of charming gentlemen asking me to dance. I dreamed of seeing a city so much bigger than Bath, alive with people and bustling with energy.'

'It isn't what you hoped?'

'It's everything I hoped for and I feel as though I

am finally alive, finally living the life I was supposed to have.'

'That's a good thing, isn't it?'

'It's all very superficial, isn't it? All of these dreams of mine.'

Sam didn't say anything so Eliza pressed on.

'I worry that one day the sparkle will wear off and I will be left too old to marry, alone and with no real way to support myself.'

'That isn't for a long time, Eliza—you're still young and beautiful and finding London life enchanting.'

'I never understood what my parents were worried about, I always dismissed their concerns. I was so focused on getting to London, to living this dream I had, I wouldn't even begin to listen to what they would say to me.'

'You don't need to choose one thing in life, Eliza. You can have lots of dreams, lots of hopes.'

For a long moment their eyes met and she saw the affection for her in his gaze.

'Everything we do in life has consequences. They may be big or small, but they are connected all the same.'

'That is true.'

'I worry… I worry that I will choose a future based on what is important to me now, rather than thinking about what I will want in the next ten years, twenty years.'

'We do not know what is coming for us. I think everyone could go round in circles, trying to predict every moment, foresee the consequences of every decision, but that is not how life works.'

'I think you are a very wise man, Lord Thannock.' Eliza stepped in a little closer, and for a moment she felt the connection between them.

'I can be foolish, too,' he said, and Eliza saw the battle on his face as he swayed towards her.

'We can't do this, can we?' More than anything she wanted to feel his lips on hers, to feel his firm arm around her waist. When she was in his arms, she felt happy and safe and desired, but she knew it was pulling Sam apart inside. He was an honourable man, a principled man, and she could see he felt as though he were risking her reputation every time they came together.

'No, we can't, Eliza,' he said as he moved a step closer. 'Every part of me wants to, believe me, but I cannot keep taking advantage of you.'

'Is it taking advantage of me if I want it as much as you?'

'I should be protecting you, not seducing you.' He reached out and caressed her cheek with his fingers, the touch making her take a little gasp of breath. 'I… care for you, Eliza, more than I have cared for anyone before, but I know we do not, *cannot* have a future together.' He shook his head, 'We want different things.'

'What if I don't know what I want?'

He nodded, his eyes searching her. 'You might not know what you want, but you do know what you don't want and that is the life I can offer you.'

Eliza nodded, even though she wasn't sure it was strictly true. Sam might not thrive in this world of balls and dinners and evenings at the opera, but he was part of it.

Ever so slowly, he dropped his hand from her cheek and stepped away. Eliza pressed her lips together, determined she would not let them tremble and give away how close she was to tears.

'I'd better wake Lady Mountjoy and head home before we are missed.'

'Good idea,' Sam said, allowing her to walk ahead of him and following at a good distance.

Chapter Fifteen

As he ascended the steps to the Mountjoys' town house, Sam was surprised to see the door open before he reached the top. He knew the footmen here were well-trained, but normally he got to knock on the door before he was greeted.

'Good afternoon, Lord Thannock. Shall I send word to Miss Stanley you are here?'

'Yes, thank you.'

'If you would like to wait in the drawing room with the other gentlemen.'

Sam blinked and stopped in his tracks, turning back to face the footman. 'Other gentlemen?'

'There are three other gentlemen callers here today, my lord.'

Sam wanted to enquire more, but knew it would be opening himself up to gossip in the servants' quarters if he showed too much of a reaction. Instead, he turned back and continued on his way to the drawing room.

As he opened the door, the three men inside shot to

their feet, obviously expecting the young women they were calling on to be entering. They all looked disappointed when they saw it was him and after giving nods of greeting returned to their seats.

Sam walked over to the tray of tea laid out in the middle of the room. He touched the pot and found it was still warm so helped himself to a cup. It gave him something to do while he studied the other gentlemen in the room.

Sitting at one end was Mr Hautby, the gentleman who had been so attentive to Eliza the night before, rescuing her when Sam had disappeared and abandoned her for their dance. At the other end of the room was Mr Miller, a young man who Sam knew had danced with Eliza at the masquerade and who was looking at him nervously now.

Sprawled out on the sofa in the middle of the room was Mr Farthington, the hapless young man Sam had saved from the ice a few days earlier.

'Good afternoon,' Mr Farthington said with a grin. 'I was hoping I might see you here. I wanted to say thank you again.'

'It was my pleasure.'

'Jolly brave, coming out on to the ice when it was cracking. It's scary stuff, deep water, especially when it is freezing cold to boot.'

Sam took a sip of his tea and tried to fix his friendliest smile on his face.

'You are here to call upon…?'

'Miss Huntley,' Mr Farthington said with a dreamy

look in his eye. 'She is quite the most elegant young woman I have ever met.'

'You know her well?' Sam had only spoken to the young woman briefly, but he knew Eliza's opinion of her.

'A little. I was lucky enough to be invited to Lady Mountjoy's house party in Somerset and I spent a little time with Miss Huntley there…' He paused and lowered his voice. 'More admired her from afar, if you know what I mean, but after the scare on the ice a few days ago I thought it was time I seized the moment and came to declare my interest.'

'You're going to do that today?'

'Yes. No time like the present. Seize the day and all that.' He swallowed hard. 'I only hope she is gentle with me.'

'You are not hopeful?'

Mr Farthington gave a little self-deprecating laugh. 'Look at me,' he whispered, motioning to his lanky form and pale complexion. 'She is a beauty, a work of art. I am…well, I am me.'

Sam could see what Mr Farthington meant by his description and leaned across and gently thumped the younger man on the arm.

'Courage,' he said, 'and a positive mindset. I am sure you have things to offer in a relationship. You do not have to be equal in every way as long as the scales balance overall.'

Mr Farthington rallied a little and was able to reach for his teacup without it rattling in the saucer too loudly.

Sam turned his attention to Mr Hautby and Mr

Miller. Without a doubt he knew these two were here for Eliza. For a moment, he wondered if he should leave, to give her the opportunity to get to know these admirers, these gentlemen, one of whom might be the man she decided to marry when they broke off their engagement. The idea left a sour taste in his mouth, and he settled back in his chair to sip his cup of tea.

Softly, Eliza closed the door behind her and leaned against it. There might be two floors between her and the gentlemen downstairs, but she didn't want to risk anyone hearing her.

'Who was it?' Lucy asked from her position on the bed Eliza and Jane shared.

'There's four of them now,' Eliza said, coming to join Lucy and Jane. 'Mr Farthington, Mr Hautby, Mr Miller and Lord Thannock.'

'Mr Hautby and Lord Thannock are obviously for you. Did you dance with Mr Miller?'

Eliza nodded her head.

'Three callers, that is incredible.'

Biting her lip, Eliza knew she should agree.

'Surely the number does not matter as much as the identity of the gentlemen,' Jane said, giving Eliza a little smile. 'It would not matter if you had a thousand callers if the right one wasn't sitting downstairs.'

Both Lucy's and Jane's eyes fixed on her, and Eliza nodded thoughtfully.

'What did happen on the terrace?'

Eliza knew that Jane had seen her in an embrace with Sam, or at the very least completely dishevelled as she came up for air. Lucy knew less, but probably in her quiet, perceptive ways had guessed more.

'Lord Thannock and I shared a moment.'

'A moment?'

'A kiss.'

Jane bit her lip. 'It looked like quite a kiss.'

'It was. It was wonderful,' Eliza said, cautious of saying too much, but unable to keep all the conflicting emotions inside.

'Have you agreed to marry him for real, then?' Lucy was looking at her intently.

'No. He hasn't asked.'

'He didn't ask after that kiss?'

'No.'

'Or when you went back to his house?' Jane clarified.

'No.'

Her friends fell silent and Eliza felt the urge to both break into tears and defend Sam's lack of a proposal.

'Do you want him to propose?'

'No. Yes. No.' She gave a frustrated groan. 'I don't know.'

'Would you say yes if he did?' Jane leaned forward, taking her hand and giving her a reassuring squeeze.

Eliza closed her eyes for a long moment and then slowly nodded. 'Yes.'

'Oh, Eliza.' Lucy threw her arms around Eliza and pulled her in for a hug. 'You love him, don't you?'

'I don't know. I just know how I feel when I'm with him.'

'Happy? Safe? Contented? As if he completes you?'

Nodding morosely, Eliza wondered how she could have allowed this to happen.

'That is love,' Lucy said confidently. 'When I first realised I was in love with William after our years of friendship it was because I recognised he made me feel all of those things.'

'I can't be in love with him,' Eliza murmured. 'We aren't going to end up together.'

'You don't know that,' Jane said kindly.

'I do. He doesn't want someone like me for a wife. He thinks we will make each other miserable after a while and a marriage between two completely different people will be doomed.'

Jane gave a quiet snort, which for her was a mighty protestation. 'That's nonsense. Even I can see you two are perfect together. What does it matter if you like dancing and he likes riding in the countryside? Life is a series of compromises and if you love someone it isn't a sacrifice to do a little less of what you enjoy and a little more of what they do.'

Eliza and Lucy looked at Jane with open mouths. Jane was quiet and kind and hardly ever spoke more than a few words at a time. They had never heard her so eloquent or so passionate.

'At least that's my opinion,' she added after a moment.

'Perhaps he doesn't care for me as much as I do him.'

'We have seen how he looks at you, Eliza. It is the talk of the *ton*. People think you've bewitched him— they say they've never seen him smile so much, laugh so often.'

A bloom of hope flared inside her and Eliza wondered if her friends might be right. She didn't want to think too much about it, didn't want to get her hopes up only for them to be dashed.

'You should go down, see what all your gentlemen admirers want,' Lucy said, giving her an encouraging smile.

'I know. It is going to be awkward, though, isn't it?'

'If Lord Thannock stays,' Jane said, helping Eliza straighten her dress as she climbed from the bed. 'If he wants you to enchant another gentleman, he will leave. If he stays it will be awkward, but you will know at least secretly he doesn't want you to move on.'

It felt like a long walk downstairs with her stomach roiling with nerves and her hands trembling so much she had to bury them in the material of her dress. She paused outside the drawing room to hear Miss Huntley's sharp voice, no doubt already irritated by the attentions of Mr Farthington. He was hardly the calibre of suitor she would be hoping to attract.

As she entered the room the gentlemen all rose to meet her, but it was Sam's eyes she sought out. He smiled at her before greeting her formally for the benefit of everyone else in the room.

'Miss Stanley, these are for you,' Mr Hautby said, stepping forward quickly and holding out a bouquet of flowers. 'I remember you saying roses are your favourite and thought I would bring you some to brighten your room.'

'That's very kind, thank you,' Eliza said, taking the

proffered bouquet and lowering her nose to inhale deeply and enjoy the fresh, sweet scent.

'I have brought you a gift,' Mr Miller said quickly, eager not to be outdone.

He handed over a beautiful box tied up with gold ribbon. Carefully, she set down the roses and untied the ribbon. Inside was a pair of delicate white evening gloves, complete with a flourish of embroidery on the fabric with her initials.

'They're lovely, Mr Miller, really beautiful.'

'I would be honoured if you would wear them to the next ball you attend—perhaps you might save me a dance?'

'Of course. It would be my pleasure.'

The other men turned to Sam, and Eliza's eyes followed.

'I haven't brought a gift exactly,' he said slowly, 'but an opportunity. I would like to invite you to an afternoon excursion.'

'Where to, Lord Thannock?'

'It is a surprise.'

'You won't give me a clue at all?'

'No.'

Eliza suppressed a smile at the idea of an afternoon of mystery with Sam.

'I can see you are busy. Perhaps I can pick you up in an hour. Is there someone who can chaperone us?'

'I'm sure Miss Ashworth or Miss Freeman will be happy to.'

'Great. I will leave you to your tea with these gentlemen.'

He stood, bowed and left the room. Eliza couldn't help but watch him go, forcing herself to turn back and focus on the two men in front of her. With Lady Mountjoy's voice in her head telling her she might need a proposal before the end of the Season, Eliza tried to be her most charming, but her mind was already racing ahead to the excursion later in the afternoon.

'Can we at least have a clue where we are going?' Eliza said, and Sam could sense the excitement radiating from her.

'No. Although I don't want you to get too excited. It's just something I want to show you.'

Eliza was tucked into the seat beside him in the carriage and across from them sat Miss Freeman and Miss Ashworth. They had been largely silent since they'd greeted him after climbing into the carriage, but he could feel their eyes upon him. He wondered what Eliza had said about him to her friends and whether they thought poorly of him after what they had seen at the masquerade.

'Thank you for intervening last night,' he said, directing his words to the two young women across from him. He held each of their eyes in turn to make sure they knew how truly grateful he was.

'We would always act to protect Eliza,' Miss Freeman said, her voice soft, but the words left him in no doubt that he wasn't fully trusted by Eliza's friends.

'Of course,' he said, deciding not to push things.

Miss Ashworth gave him an assessing look and then regarded Eliza.

'I think perhaps you would prefer it if Miss Freeman and I didn't have to accompany you,' she said, her words spoken gently, but they were blunt all the same.

'As much as I am sure your company is charming, yes. I enjoy spending time alone with Eliza.'

'Can you promise you will do nothing to further harm her reputation?'

'I can.'

'Then I think Miss Freeman and I have somewhere else we need to be.'

Miss Freeman looked at her and they seemed to communicate silently for a moment, exchanging a series of looks. Miss Ashworth must have won the exchange as Miss Freeman nodded hesitantly.

'Where would you like to be dropped?'

Miss Ashworth looked out of the carriage window. 'Here is fine, I have some shopping to do. Shall we meet in two hours for you to pick us up?'

He nodded, feeling as if he was being organised by a superior force. Miss Ashworth motioned for him to bang on the roof of the carriage and instruct the driver to stop and before anything more could be said the two young women hopped down and disappeared into the crowds.

'Did you arrange that?'

'No. I had no idea they were going to go.'

'If I'd known, I would have arranged a more exciting afternoon out,' Sam said, sitting back as the carriage moved off. 'Have you spoken to them about…?' He trailed off, motioning with his hand vaguely.

'About us?' Eliza said pointedly.

'Yes.'

'A little. Jane saw us kissing. She was naturally curious what we felt for one another.'

Sam shifted in his seat. Examining what he felt for Eliza made him feel uncomfortable and unsure. For so long he had been a man certain and confident in his decisions and convictions. He found it difficult when something came along and shook that.

'What did you say?' Sam asked after half a minute of silence.

Eliza was looking down and her expression had a hint of sadness.

'I said we cared for one another,' she said quietly.

Sam nodded. It was the truth, but hearing her say it sent a stab of pain through his heart. He knew the only thing that was keeping them apart, the only thing that would make them walk away from each other in a few weeks, was themselves. They could decide to risk their future happiness on one another. It made things even harder and he knew his heart would break a little when he had to say goodbye to Eliza for good.

'How did things go with Mr Hautby and Mr Miller earlier this afternoon?'

Eliza flashed him a curious look as if trying to work out his motivations for asking. As soon as the question had left his lips he wished he hadn't uttered it. Eliza was in an impossible situation—her reputation and her future hung by a delicate thread and one wrong step and she would be ruined.

'Fine, thank you. They were very attentive.'

'Bold to visit a woman who is engaged.'

'Fake engaged,' Eliza corrected him.

'They aren't to know that.'

Shrugging, she looked out of the window.

'Have you encouraged them?'

She sighed. 'In a way, yes. As you advised me to I have made it known to a select few gentlemen that I am not entirely happy with our engagement.'

'Did I advise that?'

'Yes,' she said, sounding exasperated. 'You said you needed to appear completely besotted and I needed to be aloof, ready to be rescued by my true love.'

'And Hautby and Miller think this could be one of them?' He hated how churlish he sounded and resolved to say no more. Eliza was right, she was only doing what he had suggested to allow her to garner the attention of other gentlemen while under the protection of an engagement to him. He didn't want to confront what his jealousy meant and instead tried to think of anything else.

For a long while they sat in silence next to one another until he felt the carriage slow and roll to a stop.

'Where are we?' Eliza was looking out of the window, confusion in her voice.

'St Augustine's. The orphanage I was telling you about the other day is here.'

'We're going to visit the orphanage?'

'Yes. I told you it wasn't a thrilling afternoon out.'

Eliza turned to him and shook her head. 'This is better than a walk through Hyde Park, or an afternoon in Lady Mountjoy's drawing room. I've been intrigued ever since you told me about supporting this place when we met that young boy in the park.'

'I spoke to Miss Hardman and told her you were a friend I wanted to show the good work they do at the orphanage. She will likely see the tour as an opportunity to try to bring you on board as a patron.'

'I'm hardly patron material.'

'Last night, Eliza,' he said, pausing before they stepped out of the carriage, 'I couldn't sleep thinking about what you said, what you have been saying to me over the last few weeks. I know you struggle with knowing what your future will hold, with not knowing what you will want in two years, five years.' He hesitated a second, wondering how to phrase the next part. He didn't want to come across as if he were saying she needed to find a worthy cause and throw herself into it, more he wanted to show her that everyone eventually found the thing that gave them purpose and happiness.

'You wanted to show me what you find purpose in,' she said, and he knew she understood.

'Not because I think this is what your focus will be, should be even, but because I thought it might help to see one of the things I've found has helped keep me interested and grounded and involved in other parts of the world.'

'It is an orphanage, but they have lessons there, too?'

'Yes, let me show you. Miss Hardman is expecting us.'

Chapter Sixteen

Together they stepped down from the carriage and walked over to the set of heavy doors to the orphanage. From the outside the building was oppressive, tall with small windows and dirty bricks, and Eliza shivered at the thought of young children calling this place home. Her childhood hadn't been perfect, but it had been a thousand times better than what these children must experience every day. She had fresh air and open fields and they had the stench of Southwark and the river and a home in one of the poorest boroughs of London.

'Good afternoon, Lord Thannock,' a tall thin woman said as she rushed to meet them at the door. 'This must be Miss Stanley. Thank you for visiting us.'

'It is a pleasure to meet you, Miss Hardman.'

'How is everyone today, Miss Hardman?'

Eliza watched the young woman as she and Sam conversed. She didn't look more than twenty-four or twenty-five, although there were lines around her eyes that aged her and her cheeks were hollow as if she didn't get quite enough sustenance. At first glance she looked severe, as if she would be strict with the children, with her hair pulled back in a bun and her shapeless, heavy black dress.

'We are in a shambles, Lord Thannock. I have had to send away our new teacher.'

Remembering what the young boy they had encountered pickpocketing in the park had said about his punishment from the new teacher, Eliza listened with curiosity.

'What happened?'

'He was over-enthusiastic about disciplining the children and focused more on that than teaching.'

'Then it was the right decision.'

'I know. I do not regret it, but it leaves us in a difficult situation. We have been through five teachers this year alone. It is difficult to get someone who is suitably qualified and shares our vision for the future of the orphanage and these children.'

'What is your vision?' Eliza was loathe to interrupt, but was keen to hear why they struggled to keep staff.

Miss Hardman seemed to soften as she perceived Eliza's interest in the children she clearly cared so much about.

'We are only small here, twenty-five children is our absolute capacity, but we hope to give those twenty-five children a chance in this world.'

Sam stepped forward and took over, a seamless exchange that made Eliza wonder how often they had given this speech to try to persuade donors or patrons to help them with their cause. 'These children have lost their parents, lost their homes, lost their former lives. We strive to give them a roof over their heads and food in their bellies, but also the chance at a future.'

'Most children in orphanages across the capital don't have a chance at a decent, productive life,' Miss Hardman said, her eyes shining. Eliza was warming to the woman and realised her stern appearance was not an indication of the person she was underneath. 'They don't get more than the most basic education and they have to work long hours for scraps you would not think fit for a dog. We are trying to change that. We do not rely on the children's income to fund anything here, disposing of the need for them to work before they have learned to read and write.'

'That sounds marvellous,' Eliza said. 'How is it all funded?'

'Donations,' Sam said grimly. 'There is a board of governors, like-minded people who help to fundraise and bring in patrons, but not everyone agrees with our way of doing things.'

'The number of people we've had come visit us and express that they think we are doing the world a disservice by focusing on the educational needs of these children. Children who are almost unanimously viewed as a burden, but who have done nothing wrong except lose their parents and their families,' Miss Hardman said passionately.

'Surely most sensible people can be convinced it is a good idea?'

Sam shrugged. 'Persuading people to donate to any cause is hard enough—persuading them to donate to something that is new or different is almost impossible.' He offered Eliza his arm. 'Would you like to have a look around?'

'Yes, please.'

They started with the downstairs rooms, currently empty. A cavernous dining hall was at the heart of the orphanage, draughty and cold, and two boys who looked about twelve were setting out the plates for dinner.

As they climbed the narrow stairs to the first floor Eliza heard the faint echo of voices that got louder the higher they rose. There were two classrooms up here. In the first was a selection of older children, all of them sitting at wooden desks and listening intently to a young man who was enthusing about geography at the front of the class. In the second classroom there was a notable lack of a teacher. The children in this room were younger, most under the age of ten. At the front of the room there was one of the older girls standing in front of a dusty blackboard writing letters slowly and carefully while the class said them aloud in unison.

A couple of the younger children turned and looked at them with curiosity, but most were engrossed in their lessons.

'They all seem very well behaved,' Eliza murmured.

'Not all, not all the time, but on the whole I think the older children in particular appreciate the opportunities we give them,' Sam said quietly. 'Many of the children arrive here traumatised by losing their parents or whoever it was who looked after them, but even more than that they are petrified by the idea of an orphanage. They have heard horror stories about institutions and are initially suspicious—it can take a surprising amount of time for them to trust Miss Hardman and the staff enough to see they genuinely want to help, that it isn't a trap.'

They watched from the back of the classroom for a few minutes and then left as quietly as they had arrived.

'The boy we saw in the park,' Sam said, too low for Miss Hardman to hear, 'has been at the orphanage for about eight months. He still can't quite believe there is no ulterior motive, no other reason people are being kind to him than because it is the right thing to do.'

Up another flight of stairs were four small dormitories, two for boys of different ages and two for girls.

'I need to speak to Miss Hardman about a few things,' Sam said after he had shown her the top floor. 'Do you mind if I abandon you for a few minutes?'

'Of course not. I will find something to occupy myself.'

As they spoke, a bell rang downstairs and there was a scraping of chairs. Eliza watched Sam go and was about to follow him when a group of young girls began to traipse up the stairs towards her.

'Good afternoon, miss,' the eldest of the group said and the three younger girls chorused after her.

'Good afternoon,' Eliza said.

'Are you with Lord Thannock, miss?' the eldest girl said.

'Yes, he has been showing me around.'

'Will you be coming to read with us, miss?' one of the younger girls asked.

'Read with you?'

'Lord Thannock comes to read to us most weeks or he will give lessons if we're short on teachers.'

'He gives you lessons himself?' Eliza couldn't quite believe it.

'My favourite was when he got us to spin the globe and put a finger on a place and he told us stories about whatever country we landed on,' the smallest of the girls said, her eyes looking up at Eliza earnestly.

'That does sound like a good lesson.'

'I liked it when he told us about all those naughty gods from Ancient Greece,' another of the girls said.

The eldest looked at Eliza shrewdly. 'He does teach us useful things as well,' she said quickly, 'like how to add up a long column of sums so we might one day aspire to a job as a housekeeper or shop assistant. Or that time he went through all the different pieces of cutlery to help Rose when she got that job as kitchen maid when she turned sixteen and was so nervous she was going to mess up.'

'They do all sound like useful things,' Eliza said slowly, 'but I can see the use in teaching you about the world or ancient history. It is important to learn to dream.'

'That's what Lord Thannock said,' the eldest girl said. 'Come on, we'd better get cleaned up before tea. Goodbye, miss.'

Three of the four girls hurried away to one of the dormitories, but the youngest, a girl of about eight, dallied and looked up at Eliza with bright eyes.

'Would you like to see something amazing?'

Eliza hesitated for just a moment and then noted the young girl's hopeful expression. 'Yes, I would.'

'Come with me, miss.' Taking her by the hand, the girl led her along the corridor, but instead of stopping at the dormitories they continued to the very end of the landing. Eliza had assumed there was nothing more past the bedrooms, but she saw she was mistaken. There was a narrow doorway right at the very end and it was here the young girl pulled on the handle and slipped through.

'What's your name?'

'Betty. Come on up, it is perfectly safe.'

With a glance over her shoulder, Eliza followed Betty up the dark stairway, pausing at the top as she waited for Betty to push open another door. Eliza was hit with a blast of cold air as Betty stepped out on to the roof of the orphanage.

Gripping hold of the door frame, Eliza followed her out. As she moved away from the door, following the young girl, she was surprised by the gusts of wind. Down at ground level it had felt a still day.

'This is my favourite place in the world,' Betty said, settling herself on a ledge and looking out over the roof-tops. The view was partially obscured by the slanted, tiled roofs of the neighbouring buildings, but the longer Eliza looked the more she thought this added to the charm.

'I can see why.'

'Sometimes I come up here and imagine all those places Lord Thannock taught us about when we spun the globe,' Betty said. 'I look out there and I imagine I can see them in the distance.'

'It is a very special place you have here, Betty.'

'I know. I love it up here. Most of the other girls don't come up—they're scared of the wind blowing them over the edge.'

'You're not afraid of that?'

Betty gave a grin that made her nose crinkle. 'My mum used to say I was like a cat. I can climb anywhere and I've never got stuck or needed rescuing.'

Eliza peered cautiously over the edge. It seemed a long way to the ground.

'So will you come and read with us, miss?' Betty asked, her face alive with anticipation. 'They're the best lessons when we have visitors. Sometimes they come in and just read a story for a whole hour. It's wonderful.'

Realising that these children didn't have parents to read to them or tell them the stories passed down generation to generation, she felt guilty about all the times she had rolled her eyes at the folklore stories her mother would tell, all of them local legends in Somerset. Now she felt a wave of nostalgia.

'How did I know I would find you up here, Betty?' Sam's voice sounded faint as it was whipped away by the wind.

'I'd sleep up here if I could,' Betty said, her voice wistful.

'Miss Hardman will certainly not allow it. You'd better get back downstairs or you might miss your tea.'

Betty's eyes widened with dismay at the prospect of missing out on teatime and she shot back to the door and disappeared before Eliza could say goodbye.

'Shall we go downstairs? It will be time to meet your friends soon before we return home.'

After a moment, Eliza nodded, but made no effort to move. Betty was right—it was beautiful up here. This might not be the most salubrious part of London—the houses were built almost on top of each other and many leaned in an alarming fashion—but there was beauty in it all the same.

'The children seem happy here,' Eliza said quietly, looking over at Sam.

'I think they are, in the main. Miss Hardman strives hard to strike a good balance between discipline and care. Of course it isn't perfect, but having set foot inside some of the alternative establishments I'm confident this one is making good progress.'

'They said you come and read to them, sometimes give them lessons?'

Sam grimaced. 'I'm no teacher, but if they are struggling I will step in on occasion. I am under no illusion the main thing I can provide to the charities and institutions I support is money, but sometimes it is nice to be needed in another way.'

'You do something that makes a real difference here.' She couldn't explain why, but Eliza felt morose. Seeing how Sam had found something outside of himself, outside of his world to contribute to was wonderful, but it made her realise how little she knew of her own dreams and ambitions. 'You're contented, aren't you?'

'Yes.' He looked puzzled at her question.

'I can't imagine feeling contented. All the time I feel

as though I am searching for more, aiming for something that is just out of my reach.'

'Doesn't that make you enjoy the moment a little less?'

'Yes, I think it does.' She shook her head, wondering how to concentrate down all the wild emotions and ambitions she felt, how to put them to a purpose that was actually useful, but also fulfilling for her as well.

'You look troubled, Eliza. That wasn't my intention and I am sorry.'

She shook her head. 'There is nothing to apologise for. I suppose I am feeling unsettled. I don't know what direction my life is going in and it makes me feel as though I am adrift.'

Sam smiled at her, a gentle smile. 'You don't have to figure everything out all at once.'

'Ah, that may be true for you, but less so for me. My choices are more limited to begin with and then will be cut down further when I have to decide whether to marry.'

'I meant it when I said I would allow society to think I have done something terrible so you can step away from our arrangement relatively unscathed.'

'I know you did. It's not only now, though, is it? I have to make the decision to marry or not in the next few years, or the opportunities to do so will dry up and it will no longer be a choice.'

She glanced over at Sam and watched his thoughtful face for a moment. Normally, talk of marriage and settling down made her feel nauseated and light headed, but she realised it would be different if it were Sam she was thinking about as her future husband. She could picture herself on his arm, strolling through the streets of London. Together they would continue his charity work, make a difference to these children, and decide what other adventures they wanted to have. Perhaps travel or set up an educational institution of their own. None of it felt so daunting when it was Sam she was imagining as her future husband.

With one last inhale of the thick London air, Eliza motioned for them to make their way back down the stairs to the dormitory corridor. Soon she would have to make a decision, and daydreaming about a life with Sam wasn't one of the options.

Chapter Seventeen

Sitting back in his armchair, Sam swirled the brandy around and around in his glass. It had been a curious day, on the whole successful, but he didn't like the hint of melancholy he had seen in Eliza's eyes as they had stood on the rooftop of the orphanage.

He'd wanted to show her that everyone found their passion or purpose eventually. Over the years he'd tried various pursuits, but always had found himself feeling rather empty. It was only when a friend had suggested he become patron to a charity that he had realised there was a whole world out there on his doorstep that he knew nothing about, a world he could make a tiny bit better for a few people.

For Eliza it might not be supporting a charity. It might be Egyptology or campaigning for women's rights or travelling the world, but he had wanted her to see that there was a place for everyone, even if it felt as though it might take for ever for her to find hers.

'I am all packed and ready for my trip,' his mother

said as she sailed into the room. They hadn't spoken much since the night of the masquerade, with his mother nursing an awful hangover for well over a day.

'What time will you leave tomorrow?'

'Early, I think. It is always such a bore getting out of London. It takes so long to get clear of the city.'

Sam kept his face neutral, not wanting to upset his mother by letting her see the relief he felt at her moving on for a few months.

'I am sorry about the masquerade,' Lady Thannock said quietly.

In all his years, both through childhood and as an adult, Sam had never heard his mother apologise for her behaviour, not when she was sober. Either she ignored it or denied it.

He nodded slowly.

'I know I have a…problem, Samuel. I know sometimes I drink too much…' She paused, perching on the edge of the chair opposite him. 'It is something that has crept up on me over the years and after a long time of telling myself I could control it, I find now it is controlling me.'

Sam didn't know what to say. His mother looked lost, sitting opposite him, and he reached out and placed his hand over hers.

'I hate to embarrass you, of course I do, but it is as though something is always driving me inside and I can't stop it.' She gave a little nervous laugh.

'I worry about you,' Sam said quietly. 'Whether you are here or elsewhere, I worry about you.'

His mother clutched at his fingers. 'You shouldn't be worrying about me. It is my job to worry about you.'

'We could enlist some help, if you wanted it? Some help to stop drinking?'

For a long moment his mother stayed silent and then she nodded. 'I have written to dearest Penelope and asked for her help. I thought some fresh Scottish air and a few months away from everything might be exactly what I need.'

'I think it will be a great help,' Sam said. Silently, he decided he would write to his mother's friend in Scotland, too, and beg for her to hide away the alcohol so his mother might have a chance at not drinking for a few months. 'We have never spoken about what happened in Italy.'

Lady Thannock held up her hand and pressed her fingers to her eyes. 'I can't, Samuel, not yet. One day when my heart has healed a little, then I will tell you everything, but not right now.'

There was nothing to say to that. It would be unfair to meddle, to press her about what had gone wrong, before she was ready.

'What about you? I worry about you and Miss Stanley. I don't think you see what sort of young woman she is.'

Immediately Sam felt himself bristle. His mother had barely spoken to Eliza, hadn't tried to get to know her. He knew much of that was his fault, he had actively tried to keep them apart, but except for a few words warning him away from Eliza she hadn't tried to delve deeper on the subject of his engagement or his fiancée.

'I know what sort of woman Miss Stanley is, Mother.'

'You're too kind, you just see the good in people.'

'There is good in her.'

Lady Thannock shook her head. 'You are an eligible man, Samuel.' She held up her hands to ward off his trying to silence her. 'I know you are not interested in marrying the wealthiest heiress or the daughter of the most influential peer, but I thought you would know better than to be tricked by a woman who has nothing, who is not even really of our world.'

'Please let us not fall out over this the night before you leave for Scotland,' Sam said, not wanting to argue over the matter, but equally not wanting to hear his mother disparage Eliza any more.

'She is not good enough for you. You could have the pick of the debutantes, any woman you desire.'

'Can we talk of something else?'

'You will be unhappy together. She will make you unhappy.'

Sam stood abruptly, not wanting to hear any more.

'I am only saying these things because I care, Samuel.'

He shook his head, reminding himself that once said hurtful words could not be taken back. There were many things he would like to confront his mother about, many hurts from many years, but he had learned as a child it was not worth it. She would fall silent and assume the role of a victim, she would twist the words in her head until she had corrupted the meaning, the sentiment and then for weeks she would mourn over the perceived loss of their relationship.

'I do not want to see you hurt.'

'I will not be hurt, Mother. It is just a ruse, a trick.' He regretted the words as soon as they left his mouth. Never had he meant to tell his mother about his arrangement with Eliza—it would jeopardise the whole thing.

'A ruse?'

'Forget it, forget I said anything. I bid you goodnight, Mother.'

'You can't tell me that and then run away.'

'Please forget I said anything.'

'You are not truly engaged to Miss Stanley?'

Sam sighed, turning back from the door. He didn't want to risk his mother not leaving for Scotland. If he smoothed this over, it might mean she didn't delay her trip for the sake of her son's future.

'I offered to help Miss Stanley out of a spot of bother after she was preyed upon by an unscrupulous gentleman. The engagement is fake and we will both step away from it in due course.'

'Oh, my darling boy, what have they got you embroiled in? This has that meddlesome Lady Mountjoy all over it.'

'It was my choice—no one pressed me to do anything.'

'You are too kind. Too gullible.'

Sam turned away and pressed his lips together, trying to maintain his composure.

'As I said, it is all under control. I only told you so you would not worry.'

'What is the plan? That one day you and Miss Stanley will break off the engagement, dragging your name through the dirt?' Lady Thannock was shaking her head in anger. 'I thought you were more worldly than this, Samuel. She has dug her claws into you and has a firm hold and, mark my words, you are not escaping from her now.'

'I do not think we should talk about this further,' Sam said, walking swiftly over to the door.

'Don't walk away from me. You need to sort this out or you will regret it for ever.'

'Goodnight, Mother. I will ensure I am up early to say goodbye in the morning.'

Sam had slept poorly, tossing and turning in his bed, unable to settle with all the worries running through his head. He had fallen into an uneasy sleep around five in the morning, dozing fitfully until it was time to rouse himself at seven.

Downstairs, he was surprised to find the house peaceful, with his servants going about their daily duties, but no sign of his mother or the frenzy that normally accompanied the preparation for a journey. He sat down for breakfast, enjoying the perfectly brewed cup of tea and the smell of toast wafting up from the kitchen.

'Your mother left this note for you,' Tomkins, the butler who had been with the family for decades, said as he handed over the folded piece of paper.

'She's left?'

'Very early this morning my lord.'

The note was folded neatly in half and Sam opened it to find just two short sentences on it.

*Farewell, my darling. One day I hope you will
forgive me and even thank me.*

Sam read the note and then re-read it, confused by
his mother asking for forgiveness. Perhaps she had spent
the night tossing and turning like him and had regretted
their argument. He didn't understand why she hadn't
waited for him to rise for the day and apologised in person before leaving for Scotland, but his mother always
had been a fan of the dramatic.

With a pang of regret, he folded the note and focused
on his breakfast. His mother was still relatively young
and in good health apart from the drinking. There would
be plenty of time to find a truce and hopefully work on
a relationship that was better for them both.

Today he did not have much planned until the evening when he was going to accompany Eliza to the
opera. He considered going back to bed for a few hours
to catch up on the sleep he had lost the night before,
but he never slept well during daylight hours so instead
decided to go for an invigorating early-morning ride.
Outside, the day was crisp and clear and there was only
a light dusting of snow left on the ground. The perfect
morning for a ride around one of the parks.

Sam was waiting for his horse to be brought round
from the stables where it was kept while he resided in
London when a harried-looking young man ran up the
steps leading to the front door and knocked smartly.

'A Mr Gould to see you, my lord,' Tomkins announced, motioning for the footman to step away with
Sam's coat while he had a guest.

'Very sorry to disturb you, my lord,' Mr Gould said, swallowing as if he were nervous to be there. 'I work for Mr Anderson at the *Morning Chronicle*, he begs your presence, my lord. He says it is a matter of great importance.'

Sam didn't count Mr Anderson as a personal friend, but he had come across the man in his charitable dealings with the orphanages and institutions he supported. He'd met the man on half a dozen occasions at fundraisers and always found him to be genuine and invested in the development of the causes he supported. What was more he had always seemed a sensible man, supremely reasonable, and Sam doubted he would send a messenger like this for anything other than something of the utmost importance. He wondered if he had uncovered a scandal at one of the institutions they both had an interest in. He debated for a moment and then reached for his hat and coat. It would cost him nothing to give the man a few minutes of his time.

The young man had come in a hackney and they took that back through the streets of London to the offices of the newspaper. Sam was impressed by the whirl of activity as they moved through the print shop and climbed the rickety stairs to the office above.

'Lord Thannock, thank you for coming,' Mr Anderson said as Mr Gould showed him into the older man's office. Mr Anderson was about fifty with a shock of grey hair that flopped over his eyes and a harried, crumpled look that made Sam wonder if he had been up all night.

'I have to admit I am intrigued by your invitation,' Sam said, looking about the untidy office.

'I know it has been a while since we last conversed. The fundraiser for St Augustine's, I think it was, last spring?'

Sam nodded.

'One day I hope we can sit down and discuss our visions for the future. I have just taken on a role as a trustee of St Margaret's and would appreciate your views on various points of contention at the orphanage.'

'I have heard good things about St Margaret's, Mr Anderson.' Sam knew the man hadn't brought him here to discuss the intricacies of sitting on the board of a charity today.

'We do our best with what little funds there are...' The older man paused. 'I could talk about the challenges of overseeing an orphanage all day, but I fear there is a more pressing matter. A very delicate matter.' Mr Anderson invited Sam to sit and poured them both a steaming cup of coffee, taking a gulp of his before continuing. 'I am in the business of printing newspapers, as I am sure you are aware. News takes many forms, but I am afraid to say some of our most popular features are not concerning politics or business.'

'Your scandal sheets.'

'Indeed.' Mr Anderson looked uncomfortable, as if not entirely happy with this aspect of his newspaper. 'We run two columns in the newspaper dedicated to the events and goings-on among the upper classes, and these prove to be very popular.'

'You must print what sells, I suppose.'

'Yes. Well, this morning I came into some information directly pertaining to you. It was not received early enough to go into today's paper, but one of my men had written it up ready for printing tomorrow. Perhaps it is best if I let you read it.'

Taking a piece of paper out of a pile stacked high, he handed it over to Sam.

It would seem all is not well in the household of celebrated matchmaker Lady Mountjoy. Her coup of the Season must be the pairing of the eligible but elusive Lord Thannock with the unknown Miss Stanley. Their engagement was unexpected, given Miss Stanley's recent arrival in London and Lord Thannock's notorious love of privacy. A reliable source close to the couple has been able to demystify the coupling, telling us the engagement is no more than a fake. Lord Thannock heroically stepped in to save the reputation of Miss Stanley when she was foolish enough to spend time alone with an unscrupulous gentleman. Of course the engagement cannot continue now the truth has come out.

Sam's hands were trembling as he read the short piece. He felt sick, both by the betrayal and by the implications for Eliza.

'You cannot print this,' Sam said, wondering how far his reputation could help him here with Mr Anderson.

'I would not do that, not to a man who has done so much for charities I myself care a lot about over the years.'

Feeling some of the fear subside, Sam nodded, his eyes moving over the words. He could even hear his mother's tone in the sentences, and he wondered whether she truly thought she was helping him by doing this.

'I will not print it,' Mr Anderson said, 'but someone will.'

'Surely no one else knows.'

'I sent my man, Mr Gould, to the offices of our rivals before he came to fetch you. At least two other papers have the story and are planning to run with it in various forms.'

'No.'

'I am sorry, Lord Thannock. I cannot stop them printing it.'

'I am grateful you were kind enough to alert me to what will be printed tomorrow.'

'I know the consequence of the printed word, Lord Thannock—once something is there in black and white it cannot be taken back.'

Sam nodded slowly, his mind whirring. He could visit every newspaper in the city and cajole or bribe them not to print the story, but it would soon get out anyway. It would take just one journalist to tell one other person and it would spread like fire across London.

Silently, he cursed his mother and he cursed himself for letting the story of their ruse slip out.

The article was heavily weighted in Sam's favour. It showed him as noble, not caring for his own reputation. Miss Stanley was painted at best naive and at worst conniving, and he knew what most of the *ton* would prefer to believe.

Worst still was the prospect that the newspapers might make their way to Somerset, to her parents, her friends, the people she would likely have to live with for the rest of her life.

'I can't let anyone print this,' Sam murmured.

'I do not think you can stop it.'

Sam stood and began to pace around the room, glancing at the piece of paper still in his hand.

'What time do you start printing?'

'Midnight.'

'The same for the other newspapers?'

'Yes.'

'Can you spread the word there is more to this story? That Miss Stanley is an innocent swept up in this mess and I will be at the opera tonight with another woman.'

'Your reputation, Lord Thannock, it will be destroyed.'

Grimacing, he nodded. He hadn't wanted things to be as public as this, but it had to be done. His reputation would recover—Eliza's would not.

Chapter Eighteen

'You seem unsettled,' Eliza said as she climbed into the carriage and took her place opposite him.

There was no time to answer as Miss Huntley climbed in behind her, followed closely by Lady Mountjoy.

'Jane and Lucy will come in the other carriage,' she said as the door closed behind her.

'Is Lord Mountjoy not coming?' Miss Huntley enquired.

'No, he hates the opera. In all our years of marriage I have never been able to persuade him to go.'

'Are you looking forward to it, Lord Thannock?'

'Mmm...' His mind barely registered the question he was so deep in thought. All day he had been trying to decide whether to tell Eliza what was going to happen this evening, what *had* to happen. Without a doubt he knew she would protest, might even go as far as to sabotage it, but he needed her to play along.

'Are you well, Lord Thannock?' Lady Mountjoy was peering at him with interest. She was another person who would be angry at him for his subterfuge after tonight.

'Is it a bit hot in here?' he said, pulling at his cravat.

Now all three women were looking at him as though he had lost his mind. He eyed them in their thick coats and warm gloves, breath misting in the icy air, and forced himself to smile, although from their expressions it must have come out more like a grimace.

Thankfully, it did not take long to get to the opera house and the queue of carriages waiting to pull up outside was quite short.

As he stepped down from the carriage, Sam saw Mr Anderson out of the corner of his eye, the newspaper man giving him a conspiratorial wink before disappearing into the crowd of people. Looking around him, he tried to identify any other journalists or writers for rival papers, but either they were not out here in front of the opera house or they blended in too well with the crowd.

'Shall we go inside? It is far too cold to be dallying out here,' Lady Mountjoy said, craning her neck to see where the other carriage with Lucy and Jane was. 'I'm sure Lucy and Jane will find us shortly.'

Eliza fell into step beside him and Sam felt her warmth as she slipped her hand into the crook of his arm. After the events of tonight she would be annoyed with him, but eventually she would thank him. This would set her free, paint him as the villain and allow her to have her Season and then follow whatever path she chose at the end of the year. It was the right thing to do, but at first she wouldn't like it.

'Something is wrong,' Eliza muttered in his ear, all the while giving a dazzling smile to an acquaintance across the room.

'Nothing is wrong. Everything will be fine.'

'You don't have to protect me. I can see the worry on your face.'

'Eliza,' he murmured, turning so he could see her face in profile, feeling his breath catch as his gaze drifted to her soft lips. The memory of their kisses struck him right in the middle of the chest and he had to inhale sharply to keep his composure. 'If anything does happen tonight, I need you to play along.'

'What are you talking about?'

'Please, trust me.'

'Tell me what is going to happen.'

'I...' He trailed off, wondering if he told her whether she would spoil his plan. 'Don't worry about it, just promise me you'll play along.'

'You're worrying me.'

He hated hearing the note of panic in her voice and seeing the furrow of concern between her eyes.

'Everything will be fine.' He quickened his pace, pulling Eliza along beside him until they were level with Lady Mountjoy and Miss Huntley. 'I have seen a friend I need to speak to. Will you excuse me, ladies?' Without looking back, he wove his way through the crowd, feeling some of the pressure in his chest subside as he got further from Eliza and her questions.

For a minute, Eliza followed Sam's progress through the crowd of people until he disappeared completely. In her mind she was running through all the possible things that could have made him so jumpy, so concerned. He was acting completely out of character, completely out of the ordinary, and it had her worried.

Play along—the words kept echoing in her head. It couldn't be anything good, otherwise he would have come out and told her straightaway.

'Good evening, ladies,' Mr Hautby said as he approached with his arms open wide to greet them.

'Good evening, Mr Hautby,' Lady Mountjoy said, ushering Eliza forward. Eliza gave a weak smile, still checking over her shoulder for Sam.

'You look lovely tonight, Miss Stanley,' Mr Hautby said, offering her his arm.

Reluctantly, Eliza allowed herself to be swept further into the opera house. She was so preoccupied it took her a whole minute before the opulence of the entrance foyer hit her.

'Beautiful, isn't it?' Mr Hautby murmured as he saw her craning her neck to look up at the crystal chandelier hanging from the ceiling. The walls were decorated in rich gold-and-red wallpaper, and two giant gilded mirrors sat on opposite walls, catching the crowd as they entered the opera house and reflecting them back and forth to infinity, making it seem as if it were never ending.

There were beautiful buildings in Bath, decorated inside and out in sumptuous style, but Eliza had never seen anything on this scale before.

'Tell me, are you looking forward to *L'Orfeo*?' Mr Hautby said.

With one final look over her shoulder, Eliza resolved to put her worry about Sam behind her and try to enjoy the evening. It had been something she had been eager to experience ever since arriving in London and now she was here.

Before she answered Mr Hautby, she took a moment to squash the little voice that told her everything was better when she did it with Sam. It wasn't relevant and it most certainly wasn't helpful.

'Yes, I can't wait. I have heard so much about it.'

'I think you will be enraptured, Miss Stanley. There is something magical about your first opera. Everyone thinks it will matter that they can't understand the words, but you realise there is power in the emotion of the music and that carries you along with the story.'

'I did wonder how I was going to follow a whole story in Italian.'

'You will, don't ask me how,' he said with a laugh, 'but you will.'

'Will you be so kind as to escort Miss Stanley and Miss Huntley to our box, Mr Hautby?' Lady Mountjoy asked as they came to the bottom of a sweeping staircase. 'I must wait for Miss Ashworth and Miss Freeman before I come upstairs.'

'It would be my pleasure.'

The conversation was somewhat stilted with Miss Huntley on Mr Hautby's other arm and Eliza was pleased when they had made it through the crowds and into the box. Eliza gasped with pleasure. They had a wonderful view of the stage with two rows of four chairs positioned looking out over the theatre. Below were the plush chairs in the stalls, which were already beginning to fill up. Everywhere you looked were well-dressed people, women in elegant gowns and sparkling jewels and gentlemen in well-tailored jackets.

People were beginning to trickle into the boxes, most standing and continuing their conversations, but some taking their seats, waving at friends and acquaintances across the void.

Miss Huntley chose the best seat, settling herself down and arranging her skirts about her.

'Are you staying with us for the opera, Mr Hautby?' Eliza turned to their companion, trying to make an effort. She might wish it was someone else here with her, but that didn't mean she needed to be rude.

'As much as I would enjoy that, Miss Stanley, I have promised my aunt I will keep her company this evening. She is seated right over there.' He waved to an elderly woman sitting on the other side of the theatre, who gave a cheerful wave back.

The door to their box opened again, and Eliza expected to see Lady Mountjoy with Lucy and Jane, but instead Mr Farthington stepped inside.

'Good evening,' Eliza greeted him, surprised to see him here.

'Good evening, Miss Stanley, Mr Hautby,' he said, his voice quavering a little. 'Good evening, Miss Huntley.' His eyes were fixed on Miss Huntley, who barely looked up to acknowledge him. 'I couldn't believe my luck when I saw you alight from your carriage tonight. I told myself it must be fate us being thrown together like this.'

Eliza's eyes widened as she watched the uncertain young man approach Miss Huntley. He was blushing furiously and his tongue kept darting out to wet his lips. Miss Huntley was now looking up at him with a mixture of horror and confusion and Eliza wondered if they were about to witness some sort of declaration.

'Grant me permission to enjoy this wonderful evening with you by my side, Miss Huntley.'

Taking a step back, she wondered if they should leave Miss Huntley and Mr Farthington alone. Miss Huntley caught her eye and gave a minuscule shake of her head, her eyes beseeching. It was the first time she had ever asked anything of Eliza, the first time she had communicated without a sneer on her lips.

'Miss Huntley…' Mr Farthington said.

'Well, isn't this nice?' Eliza said, bustling over noisily and placing herself in the seat next to Miss Huntley a moment before Mr Farthington could sit down. 'Oh, sorry, Mr Farthington, you weren't planning on sitting here, were you?'

He was far too polite to do anything other than murmur 'no' and take a step back.

Mr Hautby looked on with amusement and then clapped Mr Farthington on the shoulder.

'I dare say Miss Huntley and Miss Stanley would enjoy a drink before the performance starts. Shall we go and fetch them one?'

There was an agonising moment of silence before Mr Farthington nodded and allowed himself to be guided out of the box by Mr Hautby.

Beside her Miss Huntley exhaled.

'I didn't know you and Mr Farthignton were close,' Eliza said.

'We're not,' Miss Huntley snapped.

Deciding to stay silent, Eliza waited to see if the young woman would say anything more.

'He showed his interest when we met in Somerset. I

thought nothing of it, but he has been persistent since we arrived in London.'

'Do you reciprocate?'

Miss Huntley laughed. 'He has four thousand pounds a year.'

'It is not all about money, though, is it?'

Miss Huntley turned to her with raised eyebrows. 'Says the woman who has captured the heart of the wealthiest bachelor in England.'

'So you will say yes if he proposes?'

Looking away, Miss Huntley shrugged, and Eliza realised for all her antagonistic ways she was just like everyone else underneath.

'I would be a fool to turn him down. I would merely like a little more time.'

'I think he would be a kind husband,' Eliza said, wondering if she would be able to tolerate a marriage to a man like Mr Farthington.

With a snort, Miss Huntley shook her head. 'Kind but irritating.' She stood, brushing past Eliza's seat, pausing before she got to the door to the box. 'Thank you,' she said quietly before slipping out into the corridor beyond.

Eliza sat back in her chair. It was the most she had conversed with Miss Huntley since they had arrived at Lady Mountjoy's house in Somerset. She still didn't like the woman—she was rude and self-important—but it was interesting to see that despite her hard exterior Miss Huntley had the same worries as them all underneath.

Chapter Nineteen

Leaning forward in her chair, Eliza allowed herself to get lost in the music. It was full of emotion and with each song she felt the lump in her throat grow and the pressure in her chest increase. Even though she didn't understand the words she could follow the story—Mr Hautby had been right about that. The emotion of the music carried her along with it and she could feel the build to the crescendo at the end of the first half coming.

Next to her, Lucy had the same enraptured expression on her face and was leaning as far forward as she could without falling over the edge of the box to the stalls below.

'She's incredible, isn't she?' Lucy murmured, motioning to the opera singer who was reaching the difficult high notes without seemingly any effort.

'What it must be like to be able to sing like that,' Eliza said.

'And she's so beautiful. She must be Italian, don't you think, with that dark hair and those dark eyes.'

Eliza studied the woman and had to agree, she was stunning and probably drew a crowd whatever she was performing in.

As the last notes faded away there was a hearty round of applause before people began shifting in their seats and the whispers turned into chatter. Eliza turned around, expecting to see Sam at the back of the box having crept in at some point during the performance, but instead there was an empty seat where he should have been.

The uneasy feeling in her stomach was growing and growing. Something was wrong, terribly wrong, but she didn't know what to do about it. If Sam were there, she could confront him, confident in her ability to get the truth from him, but as it was he was nowhere to be seen.

'Abandoned by your admirers, Miss Stanley?' Miss Huntley called, their short truce over already.

Eliza ignored her, manoeuvring her way through the squeeze of bodies inside the box to the corridor outside. It was no better here. Everyone had chosen the same moment to step outside and for Eliza this meant it was impossible to see anything except the people a few steps in front of her. Deciding to take her chances, she started to weave her way through the crowd, keeping her eyes moving backwards and forward for a glimpse of Sam's familiar form and listening hard for a snippet of conversation that might be his. She hadn't seen him in any of the other boxes during the first half of the opera, but that didn't mean he hadn't been there tucked away in the shadows at the back somewhere.

* * *

It was a frustrating twenty minutes of searching and in the end Eliza had to admit defeat and return to the box without having found Sam. She wondered if he had left, if some circumstance had meant he'd had to return home, although she doubted anything but the most dire emergency would mean he would leave without somehow letting her know.

Lucy and Jane were still in the box, as was a forlorn Mr Farthington, sitting and dutifully listening to Lady Mountjoy talk about her beloved children. Only Miss Huntley was absent, probably wisely keeping away from Mr Farthington until the second half was about to start.

'I didn't get chance to tell you,' Lucy whispered as Eliza took her seat next to her friend. 'I received a letter from William as we were leaving.'

Eliza felt her pulse quicken as she searched Lucy's face for a clue of what she was feeling. Her friend was smiling, beaming even, and Eliza felt herself relax at the prospect of good news.

'His last letter must have got lost somewhere for this was written as if he had never been out of contact. He does not know when he will be home, but he assures me of his affection.'

'I'm so happy for you, Lucy. What a relief.'

'I know. I cried a little when I saw his handwriting. Is that pathetic?'

'Not at all.' Eliza reached out and squeezed her friend's hand, glad that at least for a short time Lucy wouldn't worry about her secret fiancé.

Most people were back in their seats now, and Eliza

allowed her eyes to drift across the opera house, all the time trying to catch a glimpse of Sam and a clue as to what he had been up to, what had him so worried. It meant she was looking at the boxes opposite her rather than the stage when a collective gasp rippled through the audience.

From that moment Eliza felt as though her whole world had slowed down. Turning inch by inch, she looked back towards the stage, unsure at first of what she was seeing. Lit up by the numerous candles and the grand chandelier above the audience was a couple so focused on one another they had not noticed they had crashed through the scenery and were in full view of the audience. They were kissing passionately and the man had a hand up the woman's skirt, resting on her leg.

Something inside her broke as she realised the identity of the two people on stage, just before everyone else in the audience did, too. The woman was the opera singer, the beautiful star of the show. Her hair was loose down her back and the costume she had been wearing from the first half was unmistakable.

Although his face wasn't visible, there was so much recognisable about the man. The way he held himself, the broad shoulders and straight back. Even the way he kissed felt familiar.

'No,' she whispered, the word hardly making any sound as it came from her lips.

Still the couple on the stage were kissing, oblivious to their audience.

'No, Sam,' she whispered again, fully aware of what he was doing. Even though she knew he was making this scene to save her from ruin, it didn't hurt any less. As his lips touched someone else's it sent a pain through her heart, and Eliza clutched at her stomach, letting out a low moan.

Now all eyes were on her and she felt as though she were suffocating under their gaze. She wanted to run, but her legs would not carry her, but she knew she could not watch this any longer.

It must have been only a few more seconds until the couple on the stage paused, as if finally becoming aware they were being watched, and guiltily broke apart. The opera singer's eyes widened and she ran off into the wings, leaving Sam standing on the stage alone, over two hundred people looking at him, judging him.

Eliza saw him drink it all in for a moment, saw his calculating frown, as if drawing out the moment so there was heightened anger and indignity directed at him which would mean more sympathy for Eliza.

Then he looked up at her and almost imperceptibly nodded.

She knew what he wanted her to do, but for a moment she couldn't do it. It was unfair, he shouldn't have gone down this route without discussing it with her first. Searching for a way out, for some other way to resolve this, Eliza realised she had been backed into a corner and there was nothing else to do but play along.

Letting the tears roll down her cheeks, the first time she had cried for a decade, Eliza spoke quietly but clearly, knowing her words would be repeated all over London.

'How could you?'

For a long moment, she held Sam's eye and then with a sob she pushed past everyone else in the box and started to flee. Out through the door, along the corridor and down the stairs. Her heart was pounding even before she began running and now she had to stop to take a gasping breath, doubled over with exertion and letting the sobs come bursting from her body.

What happened next was a blur and Eliza never knew whose arms grasped her firmly, who guided her out of the opera house and into a waiting carriage. Only once she was seated inside did she see the kind face of Lady Mountjoy.

'Come here, my dear,' Lady Mountjoy said, opening her arms to Eliza.

'Did you know? Did you know what he was going to do?'

Lady Mountjoy shook her head. 'I had no idea. If I did, I would have told the foolish man to not be so rash.'

'I can't believe he didn't tell me. I can't believe he did that.' Eliza couldn't get the picture of the kiss he had shared with the opera singer out of her mind. She wasn't naive—she was aware Sam had likely kissed many women before her, but it didn't stop her from feeling a pang of jealousy along with all the other emotions.

'I think his intentions were noble,' Lady Mountjoy said as she sank back into her seat.

Eliza nodded morosely. 'Of course he *thought* he was doing the right thing, the stupid man.'

'It has probably worked as well.'

'What do you mean?'

'Everyone will see you as a victim, entirely blameless. He will be painted as the villain, seducing opera singers while trying to corrupt the sweet and innocent debutantes of the *ton*.'

Groaning, Eliza allowed her head to sink into her hands.

'That is what you wanted, though, isn't it? To be free?'

She didn't have the strength to answer, instead turning to face the window and looking out at the shadowy buildings as they raced past.

Eliza wasn't sure what she wanted, but she did know she didn't want *this*. With his display tonight Sam had made sure everyone would gossip about him and his wicked nature. It would be a story that would follow him around for years. With a sick feeling in her stomach, she wondered if it would cost him his position with any of the charities or foundations he gave his time and money to.

Now she was free. In the excitement surrounding Sam's entanglement with the opera singer and her breaking off their engagement, no one would barely remember the circumstances that pushed them together in the first place. She would be able to continue with the Season, a little battered from her experiences, but otherwise unencumbered. It would be her choice at the end of it all whether she returned to Somerset or accepted an offer of marriage, if one was forthcoming. Or decided to embark on an adventure of her own. By sacrificing his good name, his reputation, Sam had given her the gift of choice.

'I want you,' she murmured so quietly that Lady Mountjoy couldn't hear her. She wanted Sam.

It felt freeing to actually admit it to herself, to empty her mind of everything else and realise the thing she had been running away from was exactly what she wanted.

Closing her eyes, she thought of every moment they had been close, every moment her hand had brushed his, every look, every kiss. She'd been too scared to admit it, but she saw now this was what falling in love looked like.

Pressing her head against the padded edge of the carriage wall, she took some long deep breaths. She might love Sam, but that didn't mean they could be together. It didn't mean he loved her.

She bit her lip, thinking of what he had sacrificed for her, thinking of all the ways he had gone out of his way to make her life a little better. It might not be love, but he certainly cared for her.

It was impossible for her to compose herself. She wanted to jump from the moving carriage and run back to the opera house and fling herself into Sam's arms, but even she knew that was a foolish idea. They needed some time alone, just the two of them, some time where they were in private with no one to disturb them, no one to overhear.

'Let's get you inside,' Lady Mountjoy said as they pulled up outside the town house.

Lord Mountjoy looked surprised to see them but did not pry, silenced by a pointed look from his wife, instead retreating to leave Eliza alone with Lady Mountjoy.

'Sit down, my dear,' Lady Mountjoy said, settling Eliza into a comfortable chair while she took a perch opposite. 'Now, I know this is a bit of a shock, but I urge you to think through your next actions. Do not do anything rash.'

Eliza looked up sharply. More than once she had wondered if Lady Mountjoy had mind-reading abilities with her astute statements and ability to predict the future. A little smile twitched at the older woman's lips. 'Don't worry, I am not going to pry. I will leave it to you and headstrong Lord Thannock to sort out your next step in this mess.'

'I don't suppose I will see him again, not this Season.'

Lady Mountjoy gave her a knowing look. 'I doubt he will call…but I am not so convinced you will not find a way to see him. I simply ask that you are careful, discreet. It wouldn't do to unravel this ruse of his by you being seen with him when you are meant to be heartbroken.'

Eliza looked at her hands.

'He thinks this is for the best, I am sure, but I worry Samuel does not realise what he could have, if he let himself.' Lady Mountjoy gave her hand a squeeze. 'I will see that Jane does not disturb you when she comes up. You get some rest, my dear.'

Chapter Twenty

It was dark backstage and damp in places, the whole area a warren of props and pieces of set from different shows. Without a doubt it was a good place to hide, a good place to wait until the crowd had dispersed completely.

'I cannot convince you to come home with me, my lord?' Maria Attuva said as she slinked around a painted wooden tree.

'No, but thank you for the offer, Maria. And thank you for your assistance tonight.'

She shrugged. 'We both got something out of it.'

Sam grimaced. It had been the part of his plan he had felt the most uneasy about. He couldn't be discovered kissing another debutante or even a merry widow—it would destroy them and he could not justify that even to save Eliza's reputation. Maria was different, though. Part of her job was the opera, singing and acting on stage, but he knew there was also a darker side to her occupation.

'Lord Webberly has approached me to see if I would accept his offer as a patron,' Maria said with a smile, 'so you do not have to feel guilty. Men follow where you lead.' She brandished the bank notes he had given her. 'Besides, for me it is a business transaction.'

He nodded, knowing his guilt would not be assuaged that easily, but grateful to Maria for trying to soothe his conscience.

'She is important to you? The woman you did this for?'

'Yes, she is.'

'Then I hope it works out well for you.'

'Thank you.'

He followed the opera singer out of the theatre, glad that the crowds had dispersed and the journalists he had invited to witness his downfall had rushed off to set the story to print for the morning papers.

Already he could imagine the headlines in the columns that dealt with society gossip.

'It will be worth it,' he muttered to himself resolutely. Of all the parts of his plan he had thought might go wrong, one thing he hadn't anticipated was quite how much it had hurt when Eliza had looked at him with heartbreak in her eyes.

As he set off through the dark streets, he revelled in the icy coldness of the air. It reminded him that the world was still as it was a few hours earlier. It was still winter in London, people were still hurrying to get home to their warm fires or to the welcoming glow of their local tavern. It was only his world that felt as though the heart had been ripped out of it.

He wished he'd had time to say goodbye. The thought of never seeing Eliza again, of never looking into her eyes as they shared a joke, of never listening to the sweet melody of her voice, was devastating. Even so, he knew it was the way it had to be. Eliza would have tried to convince him there was another way, she would have made him promise her not to do anything hurried or dramatic and tomorrow the newspapers would have printed the story of their false engagement rather than his public and scandalous seduction of an opera singer.

Of course there had been another way... Quickly, he pushed away the thought. It wasn't helpful and it wasn't even an option any more. He and Eliza had parted so any thoughts of a future together were ridiculous.

The streets were quiet as he approached Mayfair. His steps were slow and measured. Most of the snow had now melted, but there were patches of ice on the ground and in places he had to cross the street to avoid slipping.

'Tell Hughes to start packing. We leave London first thing tomorrow morning,' Sam said when Tomkins opened the front door.

'Yes, my lord.'

Even though he knew he wouldn't sleep, he went straight upstairs to his bedroom, needing to put this day behind him. Tomorrow he would leave London, leave this whole mess behind. He would retreat to the glorious countryside to tend to his wounds in peace and privacy.

It was impossible to settle to reading a few pages by candlelight, and Sam found he was prowling up and down the length of his bedroom, wishing the hours of the night away.

* * *

At some point close to midnight he must have slipped into an uneasy slumber, for he woke with a start as something clattered against his window. Initially, he assumed it must have been in his dream, but after thirty seconds there was another clatter.

In a couple of quick strides he crossed the bedroom, wincing as his feet touched the cold floorboards. The curtains were thick and luxurious, designed to keep the heat in as well as the noise and the light out, and he buried his fingers in the soft material as he drew them back.

Outside, standing in his back garden with her arm raised, ready to throw another stone at the window, was Eliza.

For a moment Sam was paralyzed, unable to do anything but stare, then, as she pulled back her arm farther, he began pulling at the latch and trying to get the window up in time. She wouldn't be able to see him in the darkness, and every time a stone hit the window she risked waking up someone else.

As he flung up the window a stone came hurtling through at speed and clattered to the floor. He had to admire her aim—if he had not opened the window it would have been another right in the middle of the glass.

'What are you doing?' he called quietly as he leaned out of the window and then shook his head. 'Don't answer that, I'm coming down.'

Taking a minute to pull on some trousers and a shirt, he then crept downstairs, thankful the servants all slept on the floor above. Hopefully they would be unaware of his midnight visitor.

She was waiting at the door to the garden when he opened it, her teeth chattering and her hands cold despite the thick coat she was wearing. As he pulled her inside he wondered how long she had been standing out there in the icy temperatures, trying to wake him without disturbing anyone else.

'What are you doing here?' he whispered as he locked the door behind her. It took all his strength not to pull her into his arms, to warm her with his embrace.

Somewhere above them there was a creak and the click of a door opening and they both froze as footsteps padded along the floorboards. Sam felt Eliza slip her hand into his and he squeezed it tight, wanting to draw her close even when he knew he should be sending her straight home.

A minute later the footsteps sounded back along the corridor and the door clicked shut. After another thirty seconds of silence Sam exhaled, feeling some of the tension in his body ebb away. It wasn't that he didn't trust his servants, but if they found out Eliza had been here in the night someone would eventually let it slip to a close friend, someone they trusted. That person would pass on the news and before long it would have spiralled through London and Eliza truly would be ruined.

Pressing a finger to his lips, he slowly crept to the stairs, pulling Eliza along behind him. They ascended quickly, aware that here they were exposed if anyone looked down from above. Sam only started to breathe easily once they were in his bedroom with the door firmly closed behind them.

His room was tidy and ordered, only the pulled-back bedclothes showing that it had been occupied recently. Everything was put away in its place and even the pile of books he kept on his bedside was stacked neatly.

'You shouldn't be here, Eliza,' he said, inordinately pleased to see her. His heart had ached at the thought he might never set eyes on her again and even though he didn't doubt parting would be hard he was glad he would properly get to say goodbye.

'How could you have done that to me?'

He blinked and then nodded slowly. 'I know it was a shock…'

'It wasn't your decision to make.'

'I didn't have time to explain everything. Circumstances had changed and there were things you were not aware of.'

'What could have changed so quickly? What could have made you take such drastic action when I had explicitly said I did not want you sacrificing your reputation for mine?'

He saw the flash of anger in her eyes alongside the pain she was unable to hide.

'Will you sit, Eliza, and let me explain?'

For a moment he thought she might refuse as she carried on pacing backwards and forward across the room, but finally, reluctantly, she perched on the end of his bed. Sam felt something stir inside him as he watched her lower herself down on to the bedsheets, even though she still had her thick coat over her clothes and she was only sitting on the end and not sprawled across the sheets.

'Yesterday I received a note from a man I did not know—the editor and owner of the newspaper the *Morning Chronicle*. He hinted it would be worth my while if I would visit him at his office.' Sam could see Eliza was intrigued, frowning at this departure from what she had expected his explanation to be. 'When I arrived he told me there was a story in the society pages, ready to print, concerning you and me.'

'No.'

'Yes. He showed it to me and it detailed our deception these past weeks. It was written heavily in my favour and painted you as the villain of this situation.'

'How did he get this story?'

Sam grimaced. 'My mother. We had a talk before she left and she expressed concern about our union. Against my better judgement I told her the truth. I did not want her going to Scotland and worrying about it—I wanted her to focus on her own health.'

'She went to the newspapers?'

'Yes, it would appear so.'

Eliza shook her head as if she couldn't quite believe it.

'I don't see how you went from there to kissing an opera singer in front of everyone in society, though.'

'The newspaper editor was a very reasonable chap. He supports an orphanage in north London and although our paths have never crossed before he knows me by reputation. He wanted to give me fair warning. He said if it were just his paper he would of course refuse to print, but he had confirmed my mother had visited other newspapers to guard against such an outcome and had given them all the same story.'

'This is terrible,' Eliza said. He had the urge to cross the room and sit down next to her, but he knew if he did that he might not have the strength to stop there.

'There was nothing I could do to stop the story being published and I knew it would be the end for you. I didn't know what to do other than divert everyone's gaze.'

Slowly, Eliza nodded as if beginning to understand.

'I had the editor of the *Morning Chronicle* spread the word that something scandalous was going to happen that night at the opera and I paid a few of the bigger papers not to run the original story.'

'You should have told me,' Eliza said, her eyes wide.

'I know you would have told me not to do anything and I couldn't have your future ruined like that.'

'It is only a Season. This will follow you your whole life. You have to live with these people.' Eliza frowned again. 'And what about the opera singer? Maria Attuva, isn't it?'

'Yes. I had been introduced before to Miss Attuva, although did not know her well, but she has a certain reputation.'

'A reputation?'

'She is very popular with certain gentlemen and is not short of offers to support her as her patron in return for exclusivity in her affections.'

'Did you promise her something?'

'No. I explained our situation and Miss Attuva is aware how important a reputation is to a young woman.'

'She did it out of the goodness of her heart?'

Sam shrugged. 'I paid her handsomely and pointed out that it would likely bring her to the attention of even more rich and powerful gentlemen, but, yes, I do think much of her motive was altruism.'

Now he had finished his explanation, he could see the whir of thoughts in Eliza's head reflected in her facial expressions. Gone was some of the defiant anger, but the sadness remained.

Slowly, knowing it was ill advised, but unable to stop himself, Sam stood and crossed the distance between them. The room was dark, illuminated by the light of one lone candle and this flickered as he moved, casting long shadows across the furniture.

'So, this is it?' Eliza said as he came in closer. 'This is goodbye.'

'It is the way it has to be, Eliza.'

'I don't want it to end like this.'

He gave a soft smile. 'It's not that bad. You will have your Season and perhaps during it you will work out what you want. Maybe it'll be to marry a man like Hautby and continue living a life in the whirl of society, or maybe it'll be to go home to Somerset and find your happiness there.' Trying to ignore the glint of tears in her eyes, he pushed on. 'Or maybe you'll have another adventure altogether.'

Morosely, she nodded, looking as though she wanted to say something, but didn't quite trust herself.

'I don't want you to feel guilty about this,' he said, reaching out and taking her hand, entwining his fingers with hers. 'It is something I chose to do and this freedom of choice for your future is my gift to you.'

For a long moment, Eliza looked up at him with wide eyes, and Sam knew in an instant it would be hard to resist what she was offering him.

Chapter Twenty-One

Sam's fingers felt soft in hers as Eliza brought his hand up to her lips and pressed his knuckles to her mouth. Every part of her upbringing had warned against her ever acting like this, but Eliza knew this was inevitable. It had probably been inevitable ever since she had left Lady Mountjoy's house and made her way across London alone and unchaperoned to see Sam.

'You need to go home, Eliza,' Sam said, his voice catching in his throat.

'I know.'

Sam took a step closer, so their bodies were almost touching and Eliza felt the heat coming off him. Slowly, she stood, shrugging off her coat at the same time and letting it fall to the floor.

'I can't leave…not yet,' she said, her voice barely more than a whisper. It was the truth, although she would never reveal to him exactly why. Her heart was pounding as she looked up, her eyes locking on his.

She wouldn't tell him how her heart ached or how

she felt as though her entire future had been ripped to shreds. He thought he had saved her—at least her reputation. He *had* saved her reputation, but it wasn't what she wanted. She wanted him. She loved him and it felt cruel that she had only realised it when it was too late.

If she couldn't have his heart, then she wanted one last memory, one last kiss, one last evening together, wherever it might lead.

Pushing herself up on her tiptoes, Eliza brought her lips to his and kissed him lightly. She heard him let out a low groan and then felt his hands on her, holding her, pulling her closer. Their kiss deepened, and Eliza felt a wonderful thrill pass through her body, heating her up from the inside.

'We can't do this, Eliza,' Sam said, making no move to stop, his lips back on hers as soon as he had uttered the words.

Eliza didn't bother to answer. She knew the consequences, knew that she would no longer be considered pure in anyone's eyes, but she found she didn't care. If they were careful, no one would ever know what had happened here, no one except her and Sam.

Sam's hands tangled in her hair and ran down her neck. It was as if he wanted to touch every accessible part of her and his fingers were setting her skin on fire. Gently, he broke away and spun her round, peppering kisses on the exposed parts of her neck and upper back, making Eliza arch with pleasure. She felt his fingers graze against the material of the top of her dress and relished the surge of anticipation as she realised he was undoing the hooks down its length.

A shiver ran down her spine as he pulled back the material, exposing her thin cotton chemise. She hadn't bothered lacing on her stays when she had dressed this evening, struggling enough as it was with the hooks that held her dress together to worry about the intricate undergarment.

Even though she knew it was coming, Eliza gasped as Sam took hold of the material of her dress and lifted it up over her head. Her instinct was to wrap her arms around herself, to cover herself even though she had a layer of cotton separating her body from the air in her chemise and petticoats, but it was the most exposed and bare she had ever been in front of anyone except her mother and sister or a maid.

Gently and slowly, as if they had all the time in the world, Sam took her hands and unwrapped her arms from around her body. He reached out and placed a hand on her waist and it felt as though he was touching her bare skin with only the thin layer between them.

As he drew her in to kiss her again, her chemise shifted and brushed against her sensitive skin, heightening the sense of anticipation and making her ache for his touch.

Together they tumbled back on to the bed, and suddenly Eliza found herself half entwined with Sam, her petticoats creeping up to expose more of her legs and her body tilted towards his.

'I've been imagining this for so long, Eliza,' he murmured, running a hand over her waist and tracing circles on her hip. He kissed her long and hard and then gripped hold of the material of her petticoats and pulled.

It took some wriggling, but soon her legs were bare and she saw his gaze turn to her chemise.

Eliza had never thought of herself as a shy person, but for a moment she felt a hint of panic at the thought of being completely naked. Sam must have seen it in her eyes for he paused for a moment, his hand leaving her leg and propped himself up on his elbow.

'It's not too late to stop, Eliza,' he said, his voice thick with desire, but she could see he truly meant it.

She shook her head. 'Don't stop. I don't want to stop, not ever.'

This made him smile, but he didn't return to touching her straight away. To show him she meant it, she sat up and with a steadying breath pulled off her chemise and threw it to the floor.

'You're beautiful,' Sam said, shaking his head. 'I knew you were beautiful, of course, but like this you're ravishing.'

Eliza saw the raw yearning in his eyes and felt a surge of power. She made him feel like this—it was she he found irresistible.

'You are still fully dressed,' she said, although it wasn't quite true. He had evidently grabbed at the closest things when he had seen her out in the garden, choosing to pull on a shirt and trousers, but nothing else.

Without hesitation, he pulled the shirt off over his head, dropping it on to the floor next to the bed. Eliza reached out and placed a hand on his chest, feeling the soft skin over the hard muscle, and began tracing small circles with her fingers. He groaned as she moved lower, her hand brushing against his waistband, and

Sam leaned in to kiss her deeply. Eliza felt her body arch as he pressed against her and then all conscious thought was lost as his hand trailed up her leg.

She wanted to grab hold of his wrist and keep urging him higher, but he seemed to like teasing her, circling up and then pulling back. She almost screamed as he shifted, dipping his head to catch hold of her nipple in his mouth and then his hand was touching her most private place and she couldn't suppress the loud sigh as it felt as though her body was being overwhelmed by sensations.

He kissed and nipped at her, all the time stroking her with his fingers so a wonderful pressure began to build inside her. She felt as though she wanted to grab hold of it, to squeeze and make it burst, but she was completely at Sam's mercy.

Without ever stopping his stroking, Sam began to trail kisses down her body, lower and lower until she was lifting her hips, silently begging him for more. She gasped as he pressed his lips against her and at the same time there was an explosion of pleasure deep inside and it felt as though every muscle in her body tensed as she tried to ride the wave of heat.

It took some minutes for Eliza to regain her senses and for it to feel as though she was no longer floating five inches off the bed. When she did come back to reality she reached down and pulled Sam up to her, kissing him deeply and then looking into his eyes.

He nodded, understanding her without the need for words, and quickly pulled off his trousers. Eliza felt herself tense as he pressed into her, and Sam must have felt it, too, for he paused, making sure she relaxed as he stroked her before slowly pushing in. After the initial jolt of pain a wonderful warmth spread through her and she arched her back, pushing him to go deeper.

She could tell Sam had been holding back, going slow for her benefit, but with her movement underneath him it was as if something unleashed inside him and he started to move faster and faster.

Again and again their bodies came together, and Eliza felt that wonderful pressure begin to build deep inside. As the waves of pleasure burst free and washed over her, Eliza heard Sam groan and stiffen and then for a long moment he held her, both of them completely still.

Eliza felt utterly contented when Sam rolled to the side, wrapping her in his arms and pulling her body close to his. It was cold in the room, the warmth from the fire that would have burned earlier in the evening dissipated, so she was glad when Sam grabbed hold of the bedsheets and pulled them up, covering them both.

For a long time neither of them spoke. Eliza felt Sam's steady breath on her neck, wondering what he was thinking. She hoped he didn't regret what they had done—that would break her heart even further. It might be completely scandalous, completely immoral, but at least she had something to treasure.

In the darkness, she felt her eyes grow heavy and she knew she could not afford to fall asleep here in Sam's bed. She needed to get home, to be back in the room she shared with Jane before the servants came to light the fire in the morning, or the alarm would be raised and everything Sam had sacrificed would be for nothing.

As her eyes drooped, she wondered if she should be brave enough to tell him how she really felt. It wouldn't make a difference, she knew that, but perhaps she should do it anyway. After everything he had done for her, surely he deserved to know how she felt about him.

Ever so quietly, her words mumbled in her half-asleep state, Eliza spoke. 'I love you.'

There was no outward reaction from the man wrapped around her naked body. She wasn't even sure if he had heard her or if he was already asleep, but Eliza was too far gone towards slumber to analyse the lack of response. With one last effort to open her eyes, she realised they were too heavy and she was too comfortable and surrendered to sleep.

Chapter Twenty-Two

It was the sound of the house stirring that awoke him. Outside, it was still completely dark with not even the hint of the sunrise coming through the chink in the curtains. He felt warm and contented and as if he wanted to lie here in bed all day without moving.

As he rolled over and felt the soft body in bed next to him he stiffened, the events of the night before flooding back.

He reached for the pocket watch he always kept by his bedside, having to hold it close to his face to make out the numbers in the darkness. It was a little after five in the morning, early but not early enough. Servants around the capital were stirring and starting their days and soon the first few workers would traipse out into the streets on their way to their jobs.

Part of him wanted to close his eyes and pretend he had never woken up, to wrap his arms around Eliza and hold her until it was too late to go back, but he knew that wasn't the answer. They had their plan and even now they shouldn't waver from it.

Allowing him one more minute to lie there and hold her, Sam squeezed his eyes shut, wondering if he had dreamed the whispered *I love you* he'd thought he had heard the night before.

If she loved him… Quickly, he forced himself to abandon that thought. It didn't change anything. They were not meant to be together. They were not suited.

He looked down at her dark hair spread across his pillow, the rosy tint of her lips and the soft skin of her cheek. A rebellious part of him questioned why he was so certain they were not well suited. As he lay there in bed, everything felt as though it was perfect if he shut out worries about the world and the people in it.

'That's not realistic,' he muttered to himself. They couldn't spend the next forty years shut away in the bedroom, ignoring the rest of the world, as appealing as that sounded right now.

'Eliza.' He shook her gently by the shoulder and was rewarded by her muttering in her sleep and rolling over and snuggling in to him. The urge to wrap her in his arms was too great, and he pressed a kiss to her forehead before trying again. 'Eliza, you have to wake up.'

This time she stirred and her eyes fluttered open. There was a moment of contentment on her face as she saw him, before it must have registered where she was.

'What time is it?' She sat upright, looking beautifully dazed and dishevelled, not noticing when the bedsheets fell and pooled around her waist. For a moment, Sam could not pull his eyes away from the creamy white skin of her breasts and the rosy tips of her nipples.

'Ten past five.'

Collapsing back in bed, Eliza looked over at him. 'Are we too late?'

'No. Let's get you dressed and then I'll take you back to Lady Mountjoy's. In the darkness with the collar of your coat pulled up and a hat on hopefully no one will recognise you. I doubt many people we know would be up and about this early in the morning.'

Eliza nodded, seeming to want to say something, but then thinking better of it.

With a pang of regret, he passed her the cotton chemise and petticoats he had deposited on the floor the night before. The material rustled softly as it brushed against the sheets, and Sam couldn't help but look as Eliza dressed. Her dress was a little more complex, with him fumbling with the fastenings he had unhooked so easily the night before.

'What about your servants?'

'I haven't heard anyone come downstairs yet,' he said, pausing for a moment to listen intently. 'If it's anyone, it will be Annie, the housemaid, getting up to clean out and set the fires. I doubt anyone else will be up yet. We can slip past her easily enough.'

Once Eliza was dressed, Sam pulled on his own clothes and boots, the whole process taking less than two minutes although he doubted he looked as well presented as when his valet laid out his clothes for him.

'We should go,' he said, hating seeing Eliza with her arms wrapped protectively around herself. He wanted to be the one to hold her, but he knew it wouldn't make the next half an hour any easier.

Eliza nodded, and together they moved quietly to the

door, descending the stairs in darkness. Eliza already had her coat on and Sam fetched his from where it was hanging, bringing an old hat of his mother's for Eliza to pull down low on her head.

'Ready?'

'Yes. Sam…' She trailed off.

'Yes?' He was conscious that the longer they dallied the more likely they would be seen sneaking Eliza back into Lady Mountjoy's house, but he paused and faced her all the same.

'I don't regret last night.'

'Nor do I, Eliza.' It might make this parting even harder, but he didn't regret it.

With a nod, Eliza turned away. He felt as though he should reach out, to tell her how he felt, but it wouldn't be helpful. She didn't know that the thought of never seeing her again was tearing him apart. She didn't need to know that he had never felt this way about someone before. Soon he would leave London and over the next few months she could shine in society while he licked his wounds in the countryside.

Outside, it was bitterly cold as well as dark. A thin fog swirled around the railings and obscured the road ahead of them. The conditions were perfect for creeping through the streets and remaining unseen.

They walked mainly in silence, side by side so every so often their hands would brush against each other, knuckle to knuckle. It felt like the longest walk ever even though it only took twenty minutes before they turned the corner and saw Lady Mountjoy's house, thankfully still dark.

Sam paused, taking hold of Eliza's hand and squeezing it tight. This was the moment he was going to have to leave her and it felt far too hard.

'Is there a way back in?'

'I have the key to the gate and to the back door.'

'Good. Will you give me a signal when you are back in your room?'

She nodded, giving him a smile that didn't reach her eyes, and then turned to leave.

This didn't feel right. He hated goodbyes and this was the worst of them.

'Eliza,' he called before she stepped out into the road.

It took her a long time to turn and he suspected she was composing herself to face him again,

Moving quickly, he crossed the space between them with three quick strides, taking her in his arms and kissing her deeply. For a long moment everything else in the world faded away and it was just the two of them again.

'Goodbye Sam,' Eliza said as they broke apart.

'Goodbye.' The word would barely leave his lips.

Eliza was the one to move away, this time turning and taking only one step before she came up short.

Across the street, three ladies and two gentlemen were standing. They were dressed in their evening finery with thick coats over the top and looking a little dishevelled as if they had spent a long night out dancing. All five of them had stopped walking and were looking in Sam and Eliza's direction.

Sam's eyes locked on to one of the women's and immediately there was a flash of recognition between them. It was Mrs Howe, a respectable pillar of society who lived a few houses farther down the road from Lady Mountjoy. The older gentleman was her husband, Mr Howe, a man Sam knew a little from dealings in Parliament. He knew they had a daughter and one of the young ladies looked around the right age, but he did not know the other two.

Immediately, Sam felt as though the whole world had shifted. All of their carefully laid plans had been dashed in a single moment. Everything he had sought to achieve with Maria Attuva, every moment of their ruse, was shattered here in the street outside Lady Mountjoy's house.

Eliza turned to look at him, panic in her eyes.

'Good morning, Lord Thannock, Miss Stanley,' Mr Howe said, taking a step towards them.

'Good morning,' Sam managed to force out. Eliza remained completely silent.

Mr and Mrs Howe exchanged a look and then Mrs Howe stepped out into the road, crossing quickly.

'It is very early to be out,' she said with a look of concern at Eliza.

'I am just returning Miss Stanley home,' Sam said, knowing there was no way to salvage this.

'I can see.' Mrs Howe looked from Eliza to Sam and then smiled. 'I remember being young and in love,' she whispered, leaning in a little closer so her husband or their companions could not hear. 'I do look forward to your wedding. Have you set a date?'

'Not yet.'

'Don't dally too long, Lord Thannock.'

Sam nodded. Really, he should be grateful to the

older woman. Some people would announce immediately what they had seen, but Mrs Howe was letting him know that she would give him the chance to make everything right. He wondered if she had enough influence over her companions to do the same.

As Mrs Howe bade them goodbye and the group carried on down towards the Howes' town house, he exhaled loudly.

'What a mess,' he muttered.

Eliza turned to him with a look of hurt in her eyes and with a sob dashed out across the street.

'Eliza,' he called, far too loud for this time in the morning.

She didn't stop, didn't hesitate and without thinking it through he followed her.

By the time he was in front of Lady Mountjoy's house she had unlocked the gate leading to the garden and was running down the path to the garden at the back. He followed, pushing the gate back so it crashed off the wall and cursing under his breath at the noise he was making.

Finally, he caught up with her at the back door as she fumbled with the keys. The hat was still pulled low over her face and with her head bent all he could see were her lips and chin in profile. Even from this limited view he could tell she was trembling and her chest was heaving as she sucked in great breaths of air.

'Eliza, stop,' he said, reaching her side the same moment the lock on the door clicked and opened and she half stepped, half fell inside.

Sam took a step in and hesitated, knowing he could

not chase her through Lady Mountjoy's darkened house, but unwilling to give up yet. At that moment there was a commotion at the door leading to the hall and it flew open, Lord and Lady Mountjoy at the front of the little group that poured into the room.

For a long moment no one said anything and then Sam quietly closed the door to the garden behind him and sank into a chair.

'I think some tea is in order,' Lord Mountjoy said after he had taken the scene in, backing out of the room and disappearing into the hallway.

Lady Mountjoy looked from Eliza to Sam and back again, for once lost for words. Then she turned to Jane and Miss Huntley who were standing behind her.

'Go back to bed and try to get a little more sleep. It has been an eventful few days,' she said kindly to the two young women. 'I think Miss Stanley and Lord Thannock have some details to settle.'

A strange calm descended on Sam as he realised what needed to happen now. For so long he had told himself a future with Eliza was simply not an option. They were too different, their priorities and desires had been too opposite, but now all options had been exhausted. There was no other way than to marry her. He thought back to the night before when he had taken her in his arms and how right that had felt, as well as the numerous times she had looked at him and a feeling of contentment had spread through him.

Lady Mountjoy bustled around for a few minutes, calling in a maid to light the fire and some candles, and then she sighed and sat down in an armchair across from Sam. Eliza was still standing, her arms wrapped across her chest. Since they had entered the house she had not uttered a word.

'My head is spinning from the goings-on between you two these last few days,' Lady Mountjoy said kindly, 'so I dread to think how you both feel. I can only assume you are at least a little bewildered.'

Eliza shifted slightly and Lady Mountjoy stood, ushering her to a chair before taking her own seat again.

'I will, of course, give you the benefit of the doubt and assume you were out in the middle of the night to confront Lord Thannock about his ill-advised plan at the opera yesterday evening.'

Eliza flashed him a glance, but nodded all the same.

'Unfortunately, I think it was all rather unnecessary now.'

Eliza shook her head, and Sam wanted to move over to comfort her, but he knew they needed to talk this through first. They all needed to be in agreement as to what happened next.

'Too much has happened: the events leading to your fake engagement, the ensuing closeness of your relationship, the scene at the opera last night and now this dash through London in the early hours of the morning unchaperoned. I do not think there is any other option.'

Nodding slowly, Sam sat back in his chair. He was relieved when Lady Mountjoy stood and made her way to the door, slipping out, but making a point to leave it ajar.

He exhaled loudly and then looked over at Eliza. She was studiously not looking at him. Wondering if she was worried he wouldn't marry her, he took another few moments to collect himself and then stood.

Eliza was finding it hard not to break down and let every emotion come flooding in. She felt as though she wanted to scream and rail at the world, to curse herself for her foolishness and to curse Sam for his lack of love for her. It all felt so unfair even though she knew she had brought this on herself.

Glancing at the door, she wondered if she could escape. If she ran upstairs, she could lock the door to her bedroom and stay there until everyone left her alone. It wasn't the most mature of solutions, but she didn't have many options left.

'I know we are two very different people, Eliza,' Sam said, crouching down in front of her. 'We have different priorities, different dreams.' He laughed to himself. 'Hell, we even want to live in different places with your love of London and mine of the countryside.'

She sniffed, refusing to cry. There was a declaration coming and Sam was about to be the generous person he was and sacrifice his happiness to do the right thing. She wished he would stop talking, wished there was a way for him to stop being so practical.

'Even so, I think we have come to a point where for a time we need to put that aside. We rub along well enough together, and despite our differences, I think certain compromises won't be too arduous.'

Eliza let out a choked noise that was halfway between a sob and a cry. Never in all the hundreds of times she had imagined someone proposing to her had she expected them to accept *won't be too arduous* as a reason to be together.

'I have no desire to stifle your life, to stop you from achieving whatever it is you decide you want to achieve, and I am sure there is a way we can both be happy.'

'You mean live separate lives?'

'If that is what you want.'

She shook her head. For a kind man he was being unbelievably cruel, or perhaps he just did not see how painful having him so close yet so far would be.

'It is not what I want,' she said abruptly, standing up and almost making Sam topple over backwards.

'What do you mean?'

'Thank you, but no, thank you.'

'You're turning down my offer of marriage?'

For a long time, Eliza couldn't answer. In the last few weeks she had fallen in love with the sweet and generous man in front of her, but she was not going to force him into marriage. It was clear by what he had just said he was not asking her to marry him out of love for her but out of his sense of responsibility and the desire that she didn't get shunned for the scandal that would follow her about.

It hurt more than she could explain, to be seen as a burden, a problem to be solved, and she refused to live her life like that. She also didn't want a half-marriage to Sam, one where they lived separate lives and were man and wife in name only. Her heart wouldn't withstand it.

'No, I won't marry you.'

He looked utterly shocked as if he hadn't foreseen this outcome as even a possibility.

'Eliza, you'll be ruined.'

'I don't care any more.'

With one last look at Sam, knowing now she would never set eyes on the man she loved again, Eliza dashed from the room and ran up the stairs, desperate to be alone.

'Eliza.' She heard Sam calling after her, but she didn't even pause, instead flinging herself on the bed and burying her face in the pillow.

Chapter Twenty-Three

Everything seemed to take a great effort this morning, but Eliza relished the mindless act of folding her clothes and packing her trunk. If she was careful, she could focus on the next item of clothing and not on any of the thoughts whirring through her head.

Lady Mountjoy had urged her to stay, pleading with Eliza to take a little time to consider what she wanted and not make any rash decisions, but everything here felt sour and Eliza wanted to leave as soon as possible. Reluctantly, Lady Mountjoy had sent one of the footmen to book Eliza's space on the coach to Somerset and now it was a rush to get packed before it left at midday.

It only seemed a few weeks earlier she had been so desperate to leave Somerset, to get away from the routine and the monotony of her daily life. Now she was desperate to be back, to see her family and go walking in the fields and woods so familiar to her. Anywhere far away from London would be good, but home would be the best place to go to tend to the wounds of her broken heart.

She didn't know what she would tell her family. No news would reach them directly of what had happened, but she didn't doubt after a few weeks rumours would start to trickle through and her reputation would be muddied in Somerset as much as in London. Still, anything was better than staying here.

'Are you sure we cannot persuade you to stay?' Lady Mountjoy said as she entered the room, bringing a pile of freshly laundered clothes she must have relieved a maid of on her way upstairs.

'No—thank you for the offer, though. You have been so hospitable.'

'I did not want it to end like this,' Lady Mountjoy said, sitting on the edge of the bed and smoothing out the bedclothes. 'Is there really nothing we can do?'

Eliza shook her head.

'Mr Hautby…'

'No, Mr Hautby is a pleasant gentleman, but I do not want to pursue things any further with him.'

Nodding thoughtfully for a moment, Lady Mountjoy regarded her with shrewd eyes.

'You love him, don't you?'

She didn't pretend to question who Lady Mountjoy was talking about and knew it was pointless to lie.

'Yes.'

'Then why don't you marry him? I know he asked.'

'It wouldn't be fair.'

'Why not?'

'He doesn't love me, and I am not what he wants from a wife. When he was asking me, he pointed out all the compromises we would have to make, all the sacrifices. He suggested we might be suited to a marriage in name only.'

'Oh, that foolish man,' Lady Mountjoy said, shaking her head.

'I know what he would be giving up to marry me. I know how important it is to him to have a wife whose values and priorities match his own. I'm not that person and I don't want him to always resent me because I stopped him from meeting whoever it was he was meant to be with.'

'You could marry the man you love, Eliza,' Lady Mountjoy said softly. 'It would save you from ruin and you would be Lady Thannock, Sam's wife. Think what you are giving up.'

'I know what I could have, but I won't do it.'

'Society is not kind to women who do not follow its rules.'

'I know. I know I will never be able to show my face in London again and I will probably be shunned in Bath, too.'

'It's not just that. Future husbands will view you differently, your options will shrink.'

Eliza nodded. She had thought of little else these last few hours, but she was resolved. Today she would leave London and Sam would be free to move on with his life.

'At least let me speak to Sam.'

'No. It will not make a difference. I am resolved, Lady Mountjoy.'

Slowly, the older woman nodded and then pulled Eliza in for a hug.

'Anything I can do for you, ever, all you have to do is ask.'

'Thank you for everything you have done. I have experienced things I never thought I would get the chance to these last couple of months and that is all thanks to you.'

'I should have looked after you better. I am sorry for that.'

Eliza shook her head. 'You are not to blame for any of this.'

For a long moment they embraced, Lady Mountjoy squeezing her tightly before finally releasing her with a sob of emotion. The older woman hurried from the room, leaving Eliza feeling drained and uncertain.

A few minutes later a footman came to carry her case downstairs and was closely followed by Jane and Lucy.

'Lady Mountjoy said it is time,' Lucy said, her eyes red from where she had been crying.

'You promise you will write?' Eliza gripped hold of both of her friends' hands. They were without a doubt the best things that had happened to her over the last few months.

'I promise,' Lucy said, and Jane echoed her words.

'Tell me everything about the Season. I want to hear it all in glorious detail. Don't go scrimping on anything because you think it might be too painful for me.'

'We'll tell you everything,' Jane said. 'You'll write as soon as you get home? We will only worry otherwise.'

'Of course. And there's no need to worry about me. I will be fine.'

Eliza hugged them both in turn, not wanting to let go.

Downstairs, Lord Mountjoy kissed her hand and even Miss Huntley was pleasant in her goodbyes.

As Eliza got into the carriage that would take her to the coach, she saw Lady Mountjoy looking as if she were coming, too.

'Please do not feel you have to accompany me,' Eliza said.

'Nonsense. It is a short trip to the coach and I want to see you safely seated and comfortable.'

With one last look back at the town house, Eliza entwined her fingers in her lap and dug her nails into her hand, trying not to show how hard she was finding her departure.

Chapter Twenty-Four

Striding through the front door, Sam pulled off his gloves and coat, handing them to the footman who was waiting patiently.

'You have a visitor, my lord.'

In the two weeks since he had been back at his country residence, he had received a handful of visitors, and each time his treacherous heart soared, thinking that it could be Eliza, that she had changed her mind.

'Lady Mountjoy is waiting for you in the drawing room.'

He took his time, straightening his jacket and running a hand through his hair before entering the drawing room, wondering if she had news of Eliza.

'My dear boy, what have you been doing to yourself?' Lady Mountjoy exclaimed as she stood to greet him. 'You look as though you haven't slept in a week.'

'Two weeks.'

'Hmm.'

They sat, Sam taking his favourite armchair and

Lady Mountjoy across from him, sipping on a half-empty cup of tea, which made him suspect she had been waiting for him for a while.

'What brings you to the country?'

'You! And that stubbornness of yours.'

He frowned. He was aware he could be quite single-minded from time to time, but he didn't see what he had done that was particularly stubborn recently.

'I never thought I would have cause to call you stupid, Samuel, but either you are too blind to see what you could have had or you do not value what I thought you did.'

'Have you heard from Eliza?'

'Yes, a brief letter to tell me she was home and safe and another a couple of days ago.'

'Has she managed to avoid the worst of the scandal?'

'People have talked of little else in London these last two weeks.'

Sam had left the capital before he could see what the newspapers had printed or the rumours had started to circulate over what really had happened between him and Eliza. Apart from a few close friends, he had refused to accept visits from anyone and it meant he was largely unaware of the scale of the scandal he was embroiled in. It suited him that way.

'What I don't understand is why you are here and Eliza is back in Somerset.'

For a moment, he toyed with the embroidery on the arm of the chair he was sitting in and contemplated how much he should tell Lady Mountjoy. He didn't want to rake it all up again—it hurt too much to think about at the best of times. Picking over it was hardly going to make that better.

'I asked her to marry me. She said no. That is all there is to it.'

'Why did she say no, Samuel?'

He blinked. Lady Mountjoy was always forward and not afraid to ask the questions others would deem too personal, but this seemed a step too far even for her.

She held up her hands. 'I think perhaps I need to tell you what I see when I look at you and Eliza. I see two people who are well matched in personality and in kindness. In Eliza I see a young woman who has made you laugh, made you dance and made you happier than I have ever seen you before. And in you I see a man who has sacrificed his own reputation to save hers without hesitation.' She paused to check he was listening. 'You clearly care for one another and I think she means more to you than that.'

Sam closed his eyes. Over the last two weeks he hadn't been able to stop thinking about Eliza. His memories of them ice skating together, playing the piano together, sinking down on to the bed together were both the happiest and most heartbreaking in his life. Knowing that he would never make any new memories was devastating, so he just kept reliving the old ones.

'I love her,' he said, so quietly he wasn't sure Lady Mountjoy would hear him. Not that it mattered—it was an admission to himself more than anything else.

'And she loves you.'

His eyes shot up and he searched Lady Mountjoy's face, trying to work out why she would say something that was so obviously untrue. It wasn't in her nature to be hurtful for no reason, so she must believe it, but why?

Sam thought through that last night together, the whispered *I love you* he thought he had dreamed. The look of sadness on Eliza's face as he had cursed under his breath when they had been caught by the Howes outside together in the early morning. He concentrated on the memory of asking Eliza to marry him and her turning him down. All the reasons why it wasn't the wisest move, the assurance they would find some way to make the terrible situation work.

'No,' he said, shaking his head. Pain and regret tore through him as he realised what he had done. 'No. No. No.'

Lady Mountjoy remained silent, not uttering a single sound as his mind began racing. He thought of all the smiles, all the kisses, all the times Eliza had slipped her hand into the crook of his arm and walked contentedly by his side.

Then he thought of all the times he had listed the reasons they would not work well together, how hard he had worked to convince them both it was the right thing to break off their engagement and go their separate ways.

'She loves me?'

'She loves you,' Lady Mountjoy said simply.

Sam stood and began pacing backwards and forward. Maybe it didn't change anything. Maybe it was just another ruffle in their relationship. They still were complete opposites, still wanted different things from life. They had different backgrounds, different upbringings, different priorities.

It doesn't matter, was all that he could think. If they loved each other, then did it matter? He had thought choosing the right person to be his wife was the most important thing to ensure a future that wasn't unhappy like his parents had been, but these past two weeks he had been terribly miserable.

'I think I should leave you to think things through,' Lady Mountjoy said.

'You don't have to go.'

'Of course I do, Sam dear, you have a trip to pack for. I wouldn't dally, though—in her last letter Eliza told me she had received a proposal.'

Sam felt his heart thump in his chest. 'Has she accepted it?'

'She didn't say, but she would be foolish not to. Word of the scandal can't be far away from Somerset now.'

'Don't come to see me off,' Lady Mountjoy said as she sailed from the room, and Sam sank back into his chair.

He closed his eyes, wondering if he should let Eliza marry her suitor in Somerset. He wondered who it was and whether they loved her. She was settling for a life she didn't want and part of that was because of him.

For a moment he wished his father was here. Over the years Sam had often missed him, even though he had been absent for much of his childhood. He wanted to ask him what he would advise, whether if given the choice he would make a different decision to marrying Sam's mother.

Even as he was thinking it Sam knew the answer wouldn't matter. For too long he had been held back by not wanting to repeat his parents' mistakes and in that time he had made too many of his own. Here he was, sitting and debating whether to go after the woman he loved because he was scared they might not be exactly the right fit for one another. If he thought about it, really thought about it, he would compromise over anything for Eliza. If she wanted to go dancing every evening, he would do it for her. If she wanted to live in London, he would find a way to make it work.

'You're a fool,' he muttered to himself and then stood and shouted for his valet.

Chapter Twenty-Five

'There, you look beautiful, my darling,' her mother said as she threaded the last of the flowers into Eliza's hair.

'Thank you.'

'I'll go and see how long we have until the ceremony is due to start and check if anything else is needed.'

Eliza closed her eyes as her mother left the room, shutting the door softly behind her. It was her wedding day, a day most young women were either excited or anxious about, but Eliza felt nothing but numb.

Ever since waking this morning, she had felt as though she were moving through honey, her thoughts and her movements slow. Somehow, she would survive the day, but it was barely mid-morning and already she was exhausted.

As she stared blankly into the mirror, there was a soft knock on the door. Thinking it would be her mother again or perhaps her sister bringing her a bouquet of flowers to hold, Eliza called for the person to come in.

'Do you mind if I come in?'

Eliza spun around, surprised to see the unassuming form of her future husband in the doorway. It was irregular, but she supposed there was no harm in it, seeing as they were in his house and in an hour they would be husband and wife.

'Please do,' she said, trying to summon a smile, but quickly returning to a more neutral expression when she felt her face twist into a grimace.

Mr Newbury walked into the room, pausing before he sat on the edge of the bed.

'Would you come and join me, Eliza, there is something I think we need to discuss.'

'Of course.' She swallowed. She hadn't told Mr Newbury any lies about why she was open to accepting his proposal when she hadn't been before, but equally she hadn't gone out of her way to explain everything that had led her to fleeing from London.

'I can't help but notice you do not seem very happy.' He held up a hand to stop her from interrupting. 'Now I am under no illusion that I am the sort of husband every young girl dreams of. I am no longer in my prime and although I am wealthy I do not have a title or the desire to whisk my young wife away to far-flung destinations.'

Eliza did manage to smile at him this time. She felt as though she had known Mr Newbury her whole life. He was a friend of her father's, a kind man who lived in a large house at the edge of the village. Her father had informed her he was wealthy and well respected and by marrying him she would be at the top of the village hierarchy when it came to entertaining.

Of course Eliza did not care about many of those things, other than Mr Newbury being kind.

'I do not know all of the circumstances around why you left London in such a hurry, and I do not feel I need to, but when I offered you marriage I hoped I could be of assistance to you.'

'Have you heard the rumours?' Perhaps he was here to cancel the wedding.

'Rumours do not bother me, Miss Stanley. I am an old man who has learnt that the less time people spend gossiping about others, the better the world is.'

'Do you truly not mind what it is I may have done?'

'Let me hazard a guess,' Mr Newbury said with a smile. 'I should imagine you fell in love with some unsuitable gentleman who was not quite ready to do the right thing and you were unlucky enough to get caught.'

'It's not all that far off the truth.'

'As I say, I truly do not care. I proposed this marriage because I thought it would help you.' He patted her on the hand. 'Of course I am not pretending I do not get something out of the match. I have been lonely for a long time, ever since my beloved Margaret died, and I would like a companion in my old age. It isn't a thrilling offer for a young woman, I know that, but I think I have certain things I can bring to the marriage—a comfortable home and a good lifestyle—that some young women would think it is worth giving up the perks of a younger husband for.'

'You're very honest, aren't you?'

'After all my years in the world I have come to the conclusion everything is better when we tell the truth.'

'I think you're right there.' For a moment, Eliza wondered if things would have been different if she had
told Sam how she felt a few days earlier. Quickly, she
pushed the thought away. Her relationship with Sam was
a thing of the past and it only hurt to think about him.

'Saying all that, I do not want you to go into this
marriage if you have any doubts,' Mr Newbury said
kindly. 'If there is someone else you think you would
be happier with or if you think the quiet and comfortable life as an old man's wife would make you miserable, I want you to tell me.'

Slowly, Eliza nodded, not knowing what to say. Of
course there was a man she would be happier with, but
he didn't want her, not in the way she wanted him to.
Would she be better off accepting Sam's offer of marriage, even though it had been made reluctantly? Perhaps they would still be happy, perhaps she could show
him over the months and years it didn't matter that
they enjoyed different things, that they wanted different things. Perhaps she could show him that their differences would be what made them stronger.

She closed her eyes. 'There is a man I love,' she said
quietly. 'But I loved him more than he loved me.'

Mr Newbury patted her hand again.

'I think I have said all I should on the matter,' he said,
rising up slowly. 'We still have time. The ceremony is
in an hour and we will need to leave for the church only
a couple of minutes before.' He paused at the doorway.
'Do consider what I have said and remember, if you
do change your mind, I will not hold it against you. I
have known you a long time, Eliza, and I do not wish

to see you unhappy, least of all be the cause of your unhappiness.'

Eliza felt weighed down by indecision. Perhaps she had been too hasty in pushing Sam away, but she refused to be a burden on him. If he had wanted her for his wife, his proposal would have sounded very different from the hesitant speech justifying why it would work despite his many misgivings.

Eliza felt as though the walls were closing in on her and had the sudden urge for fresh air. Grabbing hold of her cloak, she ran down the stairs and out of the house, glad everyone was too busy to notice the bride making a dash for it on her wedding day. Not knowing which way to go, she turned left up the lane and headed away from the village centre, diverting into the churchyard when she saw a group of people coming down the lane the other way.

Not wanting to be seen, she picked up her skirts and ran, cursing the thin slippers on her feet and sliding over the cobbles. She managed to stop once she was tucked around the back of the church and took a seat on a bench looking out over the countryside beyond with the stone wall at her back.

She grimaced as she looked down at her mud-spattered dress. It was white and gold, the gold thread shimmering in the sunlight, which was why her mother had been so keen she buy it when Mr Newbury had sent her a note with some money attached for a new dress for the wedding. Her mother had said she looked radiant in it, but Eliza felt anything but radiant. She felt sombre and downtrodden and as if she wanted to curl up somewhere safe and warm for a few months before emerging healed and a new, better version of herself.

Snorting, she dismissed the idea. Her options were either she get married today or she didn't. It was no use wondering whether she had been too hasty in turning down Sam. She had said no, and he hadn't pressed the matter. It wasn't as though he had ridden to Somerset and declared his love for her, begging her to change her mind.

Closing her eyes, she leaned back, taking in great deep breaths of the country air. Soon she would get too cold to stay out here, but for now she could endure the shivering for the feeling of freedom in the fresh air.

As she leaned back and closed her eyes, resting her head against the stone wall of the church, she heard a clatter of feet approaching. At first she thought it was going to be her mother or perhaps her sister, someone who had noticed her absence and was worried she had run away less than an hour before the wedding. The footsteps came closer, and Eliza realised they were heavier than she would expect from her mother's delicate shoes, or her sister's.

Peering around the edge of the church, Eliza saw the flash of a back as a man disappeared inside, hearing him wrench the door open and stride down the length of the church. Intrigued, she stood and crept to the door, wondering if this was anything to do with her or merely the vicar remembering he had left something he shouldn't on display in the church.

The man inside reached the front and paused just as Eliza looked inside. Her heart skipped a beat and at first she couldn't quite believe what her eyes were telling her. Then Sam turned around and for a long moment they both didn't move, their eyes locked together.

'I'm too late,' Sam said flatly as his gaze skimmed over her beautiful dress and the intricate twist of her hairstyle. 'You're married.'

She shook her head, wondering if this was a hallucination brought on by the stress of the last few weeks.

'Not yet,' she managed to utter. 'The wedding is in an hour.'

Sam let out a ragged breath and then strode down the aisle, stopping only when he was immediately in front of her.

'You're freezing.'

She realised her teeth were chattering as he guided her inside the church and wrapped his coat around her shoulders. It still wasn't enough to stop the shivering, and Eliza didn't know if it was purely from the cold or if part of it was due to the shock of seeing him here in her little village.

'What are you doing here, Sam?'

He guided her to a pew, and together they sat, Sam wrapping an arm around her shoulder and rubbing her vigorously until he was satisfied she was a little warmer.

'I heard about your impending wedding.'

'And you thought you would come and stop me from making a big mistake.'

'Well, yes, actually.'

Eliza let out a little laugh. 'Surely you have fulfilled your obligations by now. I ceased to be your responsibility a few weeks ago.'

'This man you are going to marry—do you love him?'

'No,' Eliza answered quickly, and she saw Sam's raised eyebrows. 'He is a friend of my father's. I think he will be kind to me.'

'How did we get here? With you about to marry the very type of man you vowed never to settle down with and me...'

'And you?' Eliza prompted.

'And me missing you every day.'

Eliza's eyes shot up to meet his. She didn't know exactly why he was here, whether it was to renew his offer of marriage out of a feeling of obligation, or to check she was happy enough in her choice to marry Mr Newbury, but suddenly she felt a flare of hope.

'When I asked you to marry me, Eliza, I did it poorly. I was thrown, I felt cornered as if the decisions were being taken out of my hands. It meant I focused on the wrong things.' He glanced at her and then pushed on. 'I know it sounded bad. I know it sounded as though I was trying to justify why it wouldn't be *terrible* to be married.'

She smiled softly, shaking her head. 'It was not the most romantic proposal.'

'It meant I did not tell you how I really feel.'

Trying to suppress the flicker of anticipation that flared inside her, she told herself not to get too excited. She knew Sam's views on marriage, on compatibility and wanting the same things as his wife.

'I love you, Eliza.'

It was not what she thought he would say and for a moment she was speechless.

'I love you more than words can express. I love you so much I have been in agony these past few weeks thinking I will never see you again.'

'But...'

He shook his head. 'No buts. I love every single little thing about you.' He reached out and took her hand, entwining his fingers with hers. 'I have an important question to ask you, but first I have something else I want to say.'

It took all of Eliza's self-restraint not to tell him to get to the question.

'Over the last week I have been doing a lot of thinking. I know I have been very vocal in expressing my views on marriage and what sort of people make a good match. I saw so much hurt from my parents' marriage that I decided at a young age I didn't want anything that remotely resembled the union they had.' He paused to check she was following. 'I got so fixated on it and the idea that if I were to marry it had to be to someone who shared every one of my ideals that I didn't see what was right there in front of me.'

'What?'

'You. And the fact that you could ask me to start a bookshop on the slopes of Mount Everest and I would say yes if it meant we got to do it together. I realised I am happy to compromise if it means I get to be with you.'

Eliza nodded, knowing she felt the same, but wondering if Sam had really thought this through.

'Mount Everest aside, what about those smaller, day-to-day compromises?'

'All of those events we attended together, those balls and dinners. I enjoyed each and every one of them purely because I did it with you.'

Eliza nodded, feeling the flutter of nerves in her stomach. 'You said you had a question for me.'

He smiled at her and squeezed her hand. 'Eliza Stanley, would you make me the happiest man alive and marry me?'

'Yes. Yes, a thousand times yes.'

Sam grinned and then pulled her towards him, lifting her into his lap and kissing her deeply. Eliza couldn't stop smiling through the kisses, wondering if she was about to wake up from a dream.

'I was so worried when I saw you here, all dressed up for the wedding,' Sam said as they broke apart.

'What time is it?' Eliza said, suddenly concerned.

'A few minutes to midday.'

'I need to get back. I need to tell Mr Newbury before he leaves the house.'

'Will he understand?'

Eliza nodded, thinking of the kindness in his eyes when he had come to see her earlier in the day. 'He will be disappointed, I think, but he will understand.'

'I will come with you.'

Together they left the church and then walked hand in hand along the street back to Mr Newbury's house. Outside, there was a commotion and Eliza could see her mother directing people to go off in various directions to search.

'Let's creep in the back,' Eliza said. 'I owe it to him to tell him first.'

Without being seen, they weaved their way through the garden to the back of the house and slipped in through the doors that led on to the terrace. Although she didn't know him well, Eliza suspected Mr Newbury would be sitting in his study, unperturbed by the panic that was coursing through everyone else at the house.

The door was made of thick wooden panels, and Eliza had to thump on it hard to be sure she was heard.

'Come in.' With a glance at Sam, she opened the door and entered the study.

'Mr Newbury,' she said, suddenly feeling nervous. It wasn't often she was lost for words, but this was a difficult situation.

'Eliza, my dear. And who is this?'

'Lord Thannock,' Sam said, putting out his hand and shaking the older man's as he rose from behind his desk.

'Ah. A pleasure to meet you, Lord Thannock.' Mr Newbury looked from Eliza to Sam and back again and nodded in understanding. 'Am I to surmise that the wedding is off?'

'Yes. I am so sorry, Mr Newbury. I never meant for this to happen.'

'Of course you didn't. It is a shame, of course, but who am I to stand in the way of young love.' He stood and walked out from behind his desk. 'I don't suppose the vicar will marry you two instead, what with the banns needing to be read.'

'Thank you for being so reasonable,' Sam said.

'I have known Miss Stanley since she was a young

girl and I have always felt a certain affection for her,'
Mr Newbury said, coming to a stop next to Eliza. 'How
can I object when you look at each other with true love
in your eyes?'

'Thank you,' Eliza said as the man she was meant
to marry kissed her on the cheek.

'Now I suggest you make your escape and I will deal
with the guests.'

'Are you sure?'

'Yes. Go and finalise the details of your own wedding plans. I will sort everything here.'

He ushered them back out the way they had come.

'He was very reasonable.'

'I know. Perhaps I have made an awful mistake—
unlike you he would have made a very reasonable husband,' Eliza said.

'Do not jest, Miss Stanley. You forget in a matter of
weeks you will be mine for evermore. And a dutiful
wife should not disparage her husband.'

Eliza snorted. 'I think you will be sorely disappointed if you think *dutiful* is a word that has ever been
used to describe me.'

'Troublesome. Mischievous. Impish.'

'What are you doing?'

'Listing words to describe you.'

She swatted him on the arm and then pressed a finger to her lips as Mr Newbury called for everyone's attention at the front of the house.

'How did you get here?'

'My horse is tied up outside your house,' he murmured, taking the opportunity to place a kiss just below her ear.

'Let's go.'

Quietly, they dashed down the lane, breathing easier as they rounded the corner and Eliza's house came into sight.

'Let me help you,' Sam said, boosting her up on to the back of his horse so she sat just in front of the saddle. Quickly, he mounted behind her and wrapped a hand around her waist while the other took the reins.

'This was not how I imagined my wedding day to be,' Eliza said, leaning back so she rested against his chest. Only an hour earlier she had felt an overwhelming despair at the idea of marrying someone else. It didn't seem real to be riding off into the countryside with the man she loved.

'How do you want your wedding day to be?'

'Do you know, I really do not mind as long as it is you and me standing at the altar saying our vows.'

'I can agree with that,' Sam said, leaning in and placing a kiss on her neck. 'Where would you like me to take you?'

'Somewhere warm and cosy and preferably private.'

'Have I told you I love you, Eliza Stanley?'

'Not nearly enough.'

'I love you. Now, let's go and add to our scandalous reputation, shall we?'

Epilogue

It was the second time in a month that Eliza was dressed in a new gown bought specifically for her own wedding, but this time she didn't feel that awful numb feeling—this time she had a huge smile on her face.

'Thank you for coming,' Sam said as he stood at the head of the table. He hadn't stopped grinning all day, and Eliza felt a rush of happiness when she realised she could call him her husband. 'My wife and I…' he said and had to pause as there was a cheer and a round of applause. 'My wife and I are grateful you made this trip to join us on this most wonderful day. I am not one for great speeches, so without further ado please enjoy the food and the drink and the fantastic company.'

Eliza looked down the table. They had found it difficult to decide on what sort of wedding they should have. After weeks of gossip and speculation among the *ton* in London, the whole of society was waiting eagerly to see what Sam and Eliza would do next. Neither of them had particularly wanted a large wedding and they knew lots of people would accept the invitation out of curiosity rather than a desire to see the couple happy.

In the end, Sam had acquired a special licence and they had invited a select group of friends and family to his London town house for an intimate ceremony followed by a sumptuous wedding breakfast. Every single guest in attendance was delighted to be part of the celebration and each cared deeply for Eliza and Sam's happiness.

'Can we escape yet?' Sam murmured in her ear.

'You've made one very short speech and already you want to get away from our guests.'

'I like these people,' he said, gesturing out to the friends and family seated down the length of his dinner table, 'but I like being with just you even more.'

'I like that, too,' Eliza said, turning to face her husband. 'When do we need to leave for the country?'

'Oh, erm, the carriage will be ready at three o'clock.' He had a slightly shifty look in his eye, and Eliza wondered what surprise he had planned for her. They had agreed after the wedding they would travel to his main country residence so she could become acquainted with her new home and be introduced to the staff. Eliza wondered now if he had organised a stop on the way.

'Lord Thannock, Lady Thannock, what a wonderful ceremony,' Lady Mountjoy said as she leaned towards them across the table. 'I couldn't stop crying. I knew from the moment I first saw you together this would be how it ended.'

Eliza laughed as Sam raised a disbelieving eyebrow.

'You couldn't have known. We were barely acquainted and I thought Eliza a careless girl.'

Swatting him on the arm, Eliza protested, 'A careless girl?'

'I didn't think it for long. Anyway, how could you have known we would end up together?'

'Sometimes I just get this sense, this feeling that two people would be a perfect match. I had it with my children's marriages and I had it with you.' She shook her head. 'Not that you didn't make me doubt myself along the way. I think that was the most difficult courtship I have ever witnessed.'

'Probably because it wasn't a courtship,' Sam murmured. 'It was a fake engagement.'

'A courtship dressed up as a fake engagement.'

Eliza laughed as Sam closed his eyes and shook his head. 'I never had a chance, did I?'

'Never.'

'Now I am happily married, does this mean you will turn your attention to someone else?'

Lady Mountjoy glanced down the table to where Lucy and Jane sat, heads bowed together as they discussed something quietly. They both looked happy, radiant, and Eliza felt a rush of affection for her friends.

'I may have an eye to my next match,' Lady Mountjoy said and gave Eliza a wink.

The conversation was lively around the table and for much of the time Eliza enjoyed simply sitting and listening to her friends converse with her family and everyone having a good time. There was one conspicuous absence—Sam's mother had not made the journey for the wedding. The official story they were telling people was that she wouldn't have had time to make the trip from Scotland back to London in time for the wedding, having just arrived at her friend's house.

No one else knew of Sam's mother's betrayal and the information she had given to the newspapers and Sam wanted to keep it that way. Eliza knew he was too angry to reach out to his mother right now, but time was a wonderful healer and perhaps in a few months he might feel able to write her a letter to tell her what had occurred these last few weeks.

'I think it is time we slip away,' Sam said, taking Eliza's hand and bringing it to his lips.

'Already?'

'I have a surprise for you.'

It took fifteen minutes to make their goodbyes, with tears being shed by many of their guests and many well wishes to send them on their way, but eventually they descended the steps to the waiting carriage and Sam helped Eliza up to the seat inside. Once he was settled next to her and the carriage rolled away, he pulled her into an embrace, kissing her passionately.

'I've been waiting to do that all day.'

'I have been waiting for a kiss from my husband.'

He kissed her again, keeping close even when he pulled away.

'So where are we going?' Eliza asked as she leaned her head back against his shoulder.

'You don't think we're off to Sussex?'

'No. I know you. You've been planning something for days.'

'I thought we would start with a little adventure to-gether.'

Eliza sat up straight and looked at him. 'A honeymoon?'

'A honeymoon.'

'Where are we going?'

'I have tickets for a boat to France and from there I thought I would let you decide.'

Eliza squealed with excitement. 'You have not organised anything more? We can go wherever we choose?'

'Wherever we choose.'

'How long have we got?'

'Nine months. I have made arrangements for the running of my estates and organised for people to step in with my commitments at the charitable institutions I support. Lady Mountjoy has been a great help and has even promised to go and read with the children from time to time. Your friend Jane Ashworth was also keen to get involved with the education side. I have a fantastic steward who will cope admirably for nine months.'

'I can't believe I get to have you all to myself for nine whole months.'

'It will be the best nine months,' Sam said, placing a kiss on her neck. 'Whatever we decide to do, wherever we go. None of that matters because I will be with you.'

Already planning all the places she wanted to see, Eliza rested back on her husband's chest, unable to believe they weren't pretending any more. Now, and for evermore, Sam would be her husband and no one could take that away from her.

* * * * *

If you enjoyed this story,
be sure to read the first book in
the Matchmade Marriages miniseries
The Marquess Meets His Match

And look for
A Match to Fool Society
Coming soon

And why not check out
Laura Martin's other great stories?

The Brooding Earl's Proposition
Her Best Friend, the Duke
One Snowy Night with Lord Hauxton
The Captain's Impossible Match